"I love Christmas," ᴄ
drawing his thoughts ba

"All we're missing is a little mistletoe to hang over the doorway."

She flushed, and he was tempted to draw her to him anyway, to kiss her senseless. In fact, as she lifted her eyes to his, as their gazes locked, desire flared.

He had no business following through on it, though. He didn't even know where he'd been, let alone where he was going. But if she didn't stop looking at him like that...

Oh, what the hell.

"Something tells me I've never needed any prompts." Then he stepped forward, placed his hands on her cheeks. He waited a moment, taking the time to study her eyes, her expression, checking for any sign of protest.

Instead, her chin lifted and her lips parted.

That was all the invitation he needed.

* * *

RETURN TO BRIGHTON VALLEY:
Who says you can't ___ ___ ___ again?

Dear Reader,

I hope you're enjoying the Return to Brighton Valley series as much as I enjoyed writing it. Each story shares a common thread—one character left home broken, hurt or angry, then returned years later to find true love and the families they'd always dreamed of having.

This story is no different. At sixteen, Joey Martinez ran away from his foster home with a chip on his shoulder, hoping to leave behind everyone who'd ever hurt him. And he did a great job of doing just that, going so far as to change his name! But when he's forced to return, an accident leaves him with amnesia—and wishing he could remember everything he'd once done his very best to forget.

Enter lovely Chloe Dawson, who's struggling to hold a ranch afloat for a family friend. She takes in the handsome soldier with amnesia and dubs him G.I. Doe. Attraction sparks, but life soon becomes complicated as old memories and pain resurface. Does love really conquer all?

If you're like me and you enjoy amnesia stories, ranch settings, holiday reunions, military heroes and romance, you're going to love *The Soldier's Holiday Homecoming*. So kick off your shoes, pour a cup of tea or hot apple cider and curl up in your favorite reading spot.

Wishing you and yours all the very best of the Christmas season,

Judy

P.S. If you didn't read the other stories in the series, you might want to check out *The Daddy Secret* (March 2014) and *The Bachelor's Brighton Valley Bride* (July 2014). You'll also find other Brighton Valley books listed on my website at www.judyduarte.com.

The Soldier's Holiday Homecoming

—

Judy Duarte

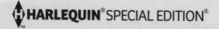

Recycling programs
for this product may
not exist in your area.

ISBN-13: 978-0-373-65849-7

The Soldier's Holiday Homecoming

Printed in U.S.A.

JUDY DUARTE

always knew there was a book inside her, but since English was her least favorite subject in school, she never considered herself a writer. An avid reader who enjoys a happy ending, Judy couldn't shake the dream of creating a book of her own.

Her dream became a reality in March 2002, when Silhouette Special Edition released her first book, *Cowboy Courage*. Since then she has published more than twenty novels. Her stories have touched the hearts of readers around the world. And in July 2005 Judy won a prestigious Readers' Choice Award for *The Rich Man's Son*.

Judy makes her home near the beach in Southern California. When she's not cooped up in her writing cave, she's spending time with her somewhat enormous but delightfully close family.

In memory of Lydia Bustos, who was called home sooner than any of us expected.
I'm rejoicing for you, Tia—but missing you, especially during the holidays.

Chapter One

Brighton Valley, Texas, was the last place in the world Joe Wilcox had ever expected to step foot in again.

Well, not when it came to the good ol' U.S.A. He sure as hell wouldn't look forward to another deployment to Afghanistan. But he'd made a promise to deliver a letter for a friend, and if there was one thing that could be said about Joe—he always kept his word.

So he'd packed a few belongings, rented a car just outside of Camp Pendleton and left California. He'd stopped in El Paso long enough to spend the night with Red Conway, a retired marine he'd met on a bus ten years ago. Red had taken Joe in when he'd been a down-and-out teenage runaway, hell-bent on leaving everyone and everything he'd once known behind.

The two men had shared a couple of beers, a pizza and a few stories. The next day, Joe had continued on for another nine hundred miles, finally arriving in Brighton Valley exhausted and hungry.

The first thing Joe did after checking in to a cheap but clean room at the Night Owl, a motor lodge that catered to travelers who were low on funds and just passing through, was to shove his duffle bags under the bed. There was a closet he could have used, but that had never felt like a safe place when he'd been a kid determined to protect his valuables from an uncle who might not have enough cash to buy a pack of cigarettes and a pint of Jack Daniels.

He probably should have shaken the habit years ago, but being back in town brought back all kinds of weird memories, leaving him a bit unbalanced.

Next he took a long, hot shower, slipped into a comfortable pair of worn jeans and a black sweatshirt and hoofed it across the highway to the Stagecoach Inn.

In spite of the seasonal chill in the air, a cold beer would really hit the spot right about now, but he wasn't looking for a drink or any entertainment. He was on a mission. He had a letter to deliver to a blonde cocktail waitress named Chloe Dawson.

Once he found the coldhearted woman who'd broken Dave Cummings's heart, he'd give her the letter Dave had asked him to deliver.

Now, as he stood on the side of the busy highway, waiting for a lull in the traffic so he could cross, he pulled out Chloe's photograph, the one Dave had always carried. He studied the photo in the flickering streetlight overhead. The snapshot was a little grainy, so her facial features weren't especially clear, but it was easy to see that the platinum blonde had long, wavy hair and a dynamite shape.

To be honest, when he and Dave had been stationed in Afghanistan, all Dave could talk about was the woman he'd placed on a pedestal and the dreams he'd had for them. Joe had been a little envious. He'd never had a family—well, not one he'd wanted to claim—so he'd never dared to consider a white-picket-fence dream. But his buddy had grown up as an only child, adored by his parents. So why wouldn't he expect to have that same life for himself?

Joe had to admit that he'd wondered what such an attractive woman had seen in Dave. Not that his friend wasn't a good person. He was kind and generous to a fault, but he'd been so sheltered by his doting parents that he tended to be naive about life and other things.

Dave had been more sensitive than guys like Joe, who'd learned early on to get tough in order to survive, and as a result, he'd been hit hard by his father's unexpected death. Then, when his mom had been diagnosed with an aggressive form of cancer nine months later, he'd been devastated.

Obviously Chloe had seen how broken up and vulnerable Dave had been and used it against him when she'd set her gold-digging plan in motion.

From what Joe had gathered, she'd rented a room from Dave's widowed mother, and when Dave had gone home on leave last summer, he'd fallen hard for her. And, sadly, he'd been too caught up in grief and lust and starry-eyed wonder to see the writing on the wall.

After Mrs. Cummings's funeral, Chloe had promised to take care of the ranch and to wait for him until he returned from war. Dave, of course, had bought her line of bull and had promised her the moon.

The dream that they'd get married as soon as he got back from deployment and eventually raise "a passel of kids" on the family ranch had been the only thing that kept him going.

Dave might have joined the Marines, hoping to man up and become independent, but he hadn't been cut out for a life of combat, especially when his idea of happy ever after was in Texas.

Not that life in a war zone had been a cakewalk for Joe, either, but growing up with an abusive drunk uncle and then ending up in the foster care system had made him both street-smart and strong. He hadn't realized it at the time, but in a lot of ways his crappy childhood had been a blessing.

Either way, Dave's defense mechanism for dealing with his depression and fears had been to cling to his future with Chloe. It was all he'd talked about, all he'd looked forward to. But apparently Chloe had envisioned an entirely different future, one without Dave. And it looked like fate had granted her that wish.

As the last headlights of the oncoming traffic passed, Joe crossed the street, his boots crunching on the graveled parking lot as he made his way to the entrance of the Stagecoach Inn, where blinking Christmas lights adorned the front window.

He could have gone out to the ranch looking for Chloe, but from what Dave had told him, she worked at the honky-tonk to pick up extra money. And Dave had spent many nights in the war-ravaged deserts of Afghanistan, worrying that some rowdy cowboy might pick up his girl while she was there.

Was that what had happened? Had Chloe found someone better looking? Someone with more money and a bigger ranch?

Joe supposed it really didn't matter why she'd broken Dave's heart, just that she'd done it—callously and without any thought of how lonely and despondent the poor guy had been.

When her Dear John arrived, Dave's depression spiraled downward. And in his grief, he'd taken off after a group of combatants on his own, a reckless act that bordered on suicide and nearly got him killed.

Joe had run to his defense and gotten shot, too, which resulted in two career-ending injuries. All because of that damn cocktail waitress. Couldn't she have waited until Dave had gone home to break up with him? Her abandonment in his time of need had led to him having a death wish, which eventually came true.

As Joe neared the entrance of the rowdy honky-tonk, the country music as well as the hoots of laughter grew louder. He pulled open the door, then paused in the doorway, allowing his senses to adjust to the smell of booze and smoke, to the blaring jukebox and the chatter of people milling about.

He was looking for a woman—a sexy blonde who'd be taking orders and serving drinks. From Dave's description, Chloe was twenty-two years old, about five foot four and a knockout. The photograph wasn't going to be all that helpful, although Joe didn't have any reason to dispute Dave's claim. Either way, in a small place like this she shouldn't be too hard to find.

Joe made his way across the scarred wood floor to the bar, which stretched across the far wall. While the bartender filled a glass of beer for a cowboy sitting three seats to the left, Joe asked, "You know a woman by the name of Chloe Dawson?"

"Yeah. She used to work here for a while, but not anymore."

"What happened to her?"

"She quit."

"Know where I can find her?"

The barkeep surveyed him for a beat, as if he was

some kind of stalker or an abusive ex-boyfriend or something. "I got no idea where she is."

Joe didn't believe that for a minute, but there were plenty of others around here who might talk. Besides, he had a feeling she was still staying out at the Cummings ranch. Why wouldn't she be? Last he'd heard, Dave had left it to her in his will.

Did she know that already? Dave had already been discharged at the time of his death, so the military wouldn't have alerted her.

How long did it take for news from the outside world to reach a small town like this?

As the bartender delivered another round of drinks to a couple at the far end of the bar, Joe pulled out the stool and took a seat. It was pretty late to drive out to the ranch tonight. Besides, the sun had set several hours ago, and he was exhausted.

When the bartender finally returned, he wiped his hands on a dish towel. "What'll you have?"

Joe wasn't sure. Did he want something strong to help him unwind and go to sleep? Or something light and satisfying to wash down the road dust he'd swallowed since his trek from El Paso?

One thing he knew for sure, he was dead tired and running on fumes, although he doubted he'd be able to fall asleep right away.

"I'll have a Corona," he said.

The bartender continued to study him. "Can I see your ID?"

At twenty-six and after eight years in the military, Joe wasn't used to being carded. But then again, he'd only been out of the service and back in the States for a couple of months. He reached into the front pocket of his jeans, only to come up empty-handed.

Where the hell was…? Oh, crap. He'd showered back in the room and changed clothes. He must have left his wallet on the nightstand, next to his cell phone and… Damn. The key to the room had been right beside it. All he had on him was Dave's letter and the photograph, neither of which would do him much good tonight.

So much for hiding his valuables out of sight. Talk about being too tired to think straight. He blew out a ragged sigh. "I'm not trying to pull a fast one. I'm staying across the street at the Night Owl. Apparently, I left my wallet there."

"Sorry, buddy. The guy who worked here before me got fired for serving a minor, and I was told to card anyone who looked younger than thirty."

"I understand. I need to get my cash anyway. Keep that beer cold for me. I'll be back." Joe slid off the bar stool and headed for the door. He felt like a batter with two strikes against him already. What else could go wrong?

As he stepped outside and made his way to the parking lot, a drunk stumbled past him, walking toward a Silverado pickup, the keys in his hand.

"You got someone you can call?" Joe asked the guy.

"Get off my back," the drunk said. "You sound like my wife."

Joe was going to argue, but a woman came out a moment later and called out to the man. "Larry, I told you I'd drive. Wait for me. I can pick up my car tomorrow. Just let me get my purse and tell Shannon goodbye. I'll be right back."

Glad the guy had a ride, Joe headed for the Night

Owl. Did he want a beer badly enough to return to the bar once he got another key to his room? He wasn't so sure that he did. Just seeing the drunken man—Larry—was a reminder of his uncle and all the nights Tío Ramon had come stumbling home, slurring his words and raising his fists, ready to strike up a fight with his aunt or whoever crossed him.

For the most part, Joe didn't drink much at all. But tonight, he might be tempted to tie one on, just like Dave had been prone to do ever since they'd both been sent to the hospital in Germany.

Dave's injuries had been pretty severe. And just thinking that he'd have to go through life physically damaged had sent the already emotionally impaired man into a depression from which he hadn't been able to recover.

Hell, Joe had been bummed, too. His own gunshot wound had made him rethink his intention to reenlist, which was why he was here now—no longer officially in the corps, but always and forever a marine.

He'd shaken his own discouragement and disappointment, focusing instead on Dave's recovery and rehab. That is, until he'd been discharged and sent back to the States. Upon Dave's arrival two weeks ago, Joe had picked him up at the airport, determined to help him mend. But Dave's depression and attitude had sunk to an all-time low, and on one of his first nights back, he downed more than his prescribed dose of meds, followed by a glass of ninety proof, ending his pain forever.

The coroner had ruled Dave's death an accident, an unintentional overdose. But Joe believed otherwise.

There was a life insurance policy somewhere, which

wouldn't do anyone any good if the death was ruled a suicide. Joe had the power to throw a wrench into the machinery and blow things sky-high, which he was tempted to do. After all, Dave had told him that he'd made Chloe his beneficiary. And on top of that, he'd left her everything—his money, his family ranch in Brighton Valley.

How lucky could a heartless woman get?

As Joe started across the street, heading for the Night Owl, the Silverado started up, but something wasn't quite right about the sound. Instead of backing out in a normal fashion, the driver gunned the engine and the tires spun, kicking up gravel as it blasted forward and over the curb.

Joe's pause to look over his shoulder at drunk Larry cost him his opportunity to make it all the way across the street as oncoming cars zoomed by him, leaving him no safe retreat as the truck shot onto the highway, barreling right at him.

He'd thought his day couldn't get much worse and might have considered this strike three, but he was too busy trying to dodge the speeding truck as it nailed him in the side, sending him flying into the night.

When Chloe Dawson received the call from the Brighton Valley Medical Center asking her to come to the hospital and identify a hit-and-run victim, a patient they believed to be David Cummings, her heart dropped to the pit of her stomach, and her grip on the receiver tightened. "Is he...*dead?*"

"No, he's unconscious."

"I'll be right there."

The moment she hung up, she threw on a pair of

jeans, a white T-shirt and sweater. Then she climbed into one of the ranch pickups and drove to town, her hands clammy as they struggled to control both the steering wheel and the gearshift at the same time, her knee wobbly as she stepped on the clutch.

Thank God her dad had insisted she learn to drive a stick when she'd turned sixteen, although this beat-up old GMC wasn't anything like the little Honda Civic she'd once driven.

She kept her eyes on the darkened country road until she reached city limits twenty minutes later and turned down the highway that led to the medical center. She snagged the first parking space she could find and rushed to the E.R. entrance.

Once inside, she told the receptionist to alert Dr. Betsy Nielson of her arrival. It gave her some comfort to know that Dave was under the care of one of the best doctors at BVMC.

After making several visits to the emergency department with Teresa Cummings, Dave's mother, and also with some of the elderly residents at the Sheltering Arms Rest Home, where Chloe had once worked as a nurse's aide, Dr. Betsy Nielson and Chloe had become well acquainted.

Fortunately, within a matter of minutes, Betsy, an attractive redhead wearing a pair of light blue scrubs came out to the waiting room personally to find her. "Thanks for coming in, Chloe."

"No problem. I'm glad you called. How is he?"

"He's conscious now, but I'm afraid he's not going to be any help. He has amnesia—and no ID."

"And you think it's Dave?"

"I've never met Teresa's son, so I have no idea what

he looks like. But the patient is in his mid- to late-twenties. A tattoo of the marine insignia on his left biceps indicates he is or was in the military. So I made the assumption. Sheriff Hollister is checking into that."

Chloe hadn't heard from Dave in months—not since she'd had to take a direct approach and tell him that a couple of shared dinners in the hospital cafeteria didn't mean they were altar-bound. She'd felt badly about hurting him, especially with him being so far from home, but each letter he'd sent her from Afghanistan had included more and more marriage plans. And she'd needed to make it clear that she only wanted to be friends.

"How badly is he hurt?" Chloe asked. "Is he going to be okay?"

"He's bruised, with cuts and lacerations. But there aren't any broken bones. His most serious injury appears to be a concussion."

"Where did it happen?"

"On the highway outside the Stagecoach Inn."

Chloe had worked at the honky-tonk for a while, hoping to earn some spare cash so she could go back to nursing school once Dave got back home and was able to run the ranch himself. But she'd never liked getting involved in confrontations and tried to avoid them at all costs. Needless to say, she'd gotten tired of having to put some of the rowdier patrons in their places as the night wore on. So she'd quit last month.

"Did anyone inside the Stagecoach Inn know who he was? I mean, Dave wasn't much of a drinker—unless that changed while he was deployed." Had he stopped by the bar to look for her? He hadn't liked the idea of her working there, but since he'd quit writing to her and her last letter to him had been returned, he might not know that she'd quit.

"From what I understand," Betsy said, "he might have gone inside, but he never ordered a drink."

"So what happened? How'd he get hit by a car?"

"The sheriff's department is still investigating, so I'm not entirely sure. Apparently he was on foot. A bystander heard the squealing wheels and the thud, but only caught sight of the taillights of the vehicle. She called 9-1-1, and he was rushed to the hospital. But because he has no wallet, the only clue to his identity was the letter he was carrying."

"The letter?"

"Apparently it was written by Dave Cummings and addressed to you. That's why I called the ranch and wanted you to give us a positive ID."

"Where is he?" Chloe asked. "Can I see him?"

"Of course. Come with me."

The doctor led Chloe through the E.R. door and along a maze of exam rooms until she reached a small area just off the nurses' station and slowed to a stop. "He's right here." She pulled the curtain back.

But when Chloe spotted the man lying in bed and took in his dark hair—clipped short but not in the customary military high and tight—as well as his olive complexion and square cut jaw, she froze in her tracks. His eyes were closed, and he had a couple of scrapes on a notably handsome face.

While she'd like to be of help to the doctor, she realized that she wouldn't be. "I'm sorry, Betsy, but that's not Dave Cummings."

"Do you know who he is?"

"I've never seen him before." She certainly would

have remembered if she had. Even asleep and with bumps and bruises, the man definitely aroused a woman's soul and would leave a lasting impression.

Upon hearing their voices, he stirred. When his eyes opened, her breath caught at the sight of their stunning sky-blue color.

He zeroed in on her, and his brow furrowed. "Who are you?"

"My name's Chloe Dawson. You had a letter addressed to me."

He merely studied her, his gaze laced with confusion.

"Do you know Dave Cummings?" she asked.

"I suppose I should, since they tell me that's who wrote the letter I had in my pocket. But the name doesn't ring a bell." He reached up and stroked his head, massaging the temple.

"You could be one of Dave's friends," Chloe said. "I'd have to ask him, but I'm not sure how to get in touch with him. He was in Afghanistan the last I heard, although he could be back in the States now."

The handsome but wounded marine looked at the doctor, then back to Chloe. "Apparently, my brains were scrambled in that accident. And the pain medication the nurse gave me is really kicking in."

"Good," Betsy said. "Maybe you'll wake up fresh in the morning and remember who you are and what you're doing in Brighton Valley."

"About that letter that was addressed to me," Chloe said. "I'd like to see it. To be honest, I haven't heard from Dave in months, and I've been worried about him."

"I don't have it. The paramedics told me about it when they brought him in. From what I understand, the sheriff is using it as part of his investigation."

"You mean he thinks that letter may give him a clue as to who the driver was?" Chloe asked. "That doesn't make sense."

"It was probably just a random hit-and-run. But they want to rule out any criminal motivation."

Chloe stiffened. Had there been a crime committed? Had the handsome G.I. Doe done something illegal?

As if sensing Chloe's concern, Dr. Nielson placed a comforting hand on her shoulder. "I'm sure there's nothing to worry about. Sheriff Hollister used to be a detective with the Houston Police Department, so he's just being thorough. He's going to check with any witnesses or people working at any of the nearby businesses. He'll get to the bottom of this—probably by morning, if not sooner."

Chloe hoped so. She couldn't imagine how the poor guy must feel—injured, alone, confused.

"If the letter doesn't give us a clue to his identity," Chloe said, "it might let us know where we can find Dave. He ought to be able to shed some light on the problem."

"So I take it I'm the problem you're trying to solve," the handsome marine said. "That's a little unsettling."

"I didn't mean to imply that." Chloe eased closer to the bed. "Besides, I'd think that you'd want to get to the bottom of this."

"To say the least." G.I. Doe blew out a weary sigh. "So how do you know that guy—Dave Cummings?"

"I'm a family friend. I live on his ranch and have been house-sitting until he comes home. That's all."

Betsy glanced at the chart in her hand, then back to Chloe. "If you'll excuse me, I'm going to complete the paperwork to have him admitted for the night."

"All right. But under the circumstances—and assuming that he's a friend of Dave's—will you make a note of my name and number in his paperwork? I'd like to be kept informed about his condition."

The doctor addressed her injured patient. "Do you have a problem with that?"

"As long as you don't list her as next of kin, I'm okay with it."

"Why would it bother you to think that I was related to you?" Chloe asked.

A slow grin stretched across his face. "Because you're too damn pretty. If we were related by blood, I'd have to fight the guys off you—rather than fight to be at the top of your consideration list."

"Would you, now." So G.I. Doe was not only handsome, but a flirt. She glanced at his left hand, checking for a ring and not finding one.

Not that it mattered if he was already taken. She had enough on her plate these days without stressing over a romance.

Still, he was more than a little attractive, even in his injured state. But she wouldn't think about that now. The important thing was that he was her only link to Dave. And until Dave came home and could take over the ranch, Chloe was stuck in limbo and unable to get on with the future she had planned.

Chapter Two

The ranch foreman, Tomas Hernandez, had just left for the day when Chloe's cell phone vibrated in her pocket. She recognized the number to the Brighton Valley Medical Center and slid her finger across the screen. "Hello?"

"Chloe? This is Dr. Betsy Nielsen. Joe Wilcox is in stable condition and we're going to be discharging him soon."

She switched the phone to her other ear, thinking she hadn't heard correctly. *"Who?"*

"Joe Wilcox. The hit-and-run patient you came in to see last night."

"His memory returned?"

"No, I'm afraid it hasn't. Sheriff Hollister called shortly after you left the hospital last night. During the investigation, he learned who our patient is. Apparently, Mr. Joseph Wilcox arrived in town yesterday evening and checked into the Night Owl Motel. When the manager let the sheriff into his room, they found his wallet and the keys to a rental car, which also had been leased to Joseph Wilcox. The name on his California driver's license is a match, as well. I was told the photo bears his likeness. But they've yet to uncover any other information, so they still don't know much about him—or why he's in Texas."

Dave mentioned something about a buddy in the corps named Joe. The last name might have been Wilcox, but she wasn't sure.

"A deputy took his fingerprints," the doctor added, "Apparently he has a military record, although it will take more time to get any classified information. Unfortunately, we don't know how long that will be. And, like I said, physically, he's stable. So there's no legitimate reason for me to keep him another night."

Chloe knew Betsy wouldn't release a patient before it was wise to do so, but she didn't have the same confidence in the hospital administration who might be worried about him not being able to pay the bill. Her experience with the administrator of the Sheltering Arms Rest Home gave her cause to worry.

"Surely the hospital won't turn him out on the street," Chloe said. "He has no memory, nowhere to go and no one to take care of him."

"Of course not. That's why I called you. Since you left your name and number as his emergency contact, I was hoping that we could release him into your care."

Chloe didn't want to say no. After all, helping people was her natural calling, an intrinsic part of who she was. But she was living in the ranch house alone. And the man was a stranger.

"If you'd rather not take on the responsibility," Betsy said, "I understand."

Chloe might not know anything about the man, but he either was or had been a marine. And he had to be Dave's friend. Why else would he be delivering a letter to her?

"What time is he scheduled to be discharged?" She still needed to finish up her evening chores, and it was already pushing five o'clock.

"He should have been released a couple of hours ago, but I stalled the admin assistant until I had time to call you personally."

So much for finishing her chores before dark. She walked to the row of hooks just inside the back door and grabbed a red barn jacket to ward off the winter chill. "Then I'll leave now."

"That's great. He's on the third floor, in room 327. I'll have the paperwork ready for his discharge."

Five minutes later, Chloe climbed into the faded green GMC pickup and turned on the ignition. The old ranch truck roared to life, just as dependable as Chloe herself.

To be honest, she was apprehensive about taking in a stranger, but she chided herself as quickly as the thought crossed her mind. Teresa Cummings, Dave's mom, had let Chloe move to the Rocking C when she didn't have anywhere else to go. So taking in Joe Wilcox was her way of paying it forward. Besides that, Teresa would have taken the wounded marine under her wing in a heartbeat.

One night, before Teresa's death, she and Chloe had shared a pot of tea and talked about Teresa's terminal illness, her fears and her thoughts on life. The dying woman had also shared her regrets, one of which was about a kid she'd neglected to take in and offer a home.

Apparently, years ago, when Dave had been in high school, one of his friends had needed a home. The teenager had been living in foster care and had been miserable. So Teresa had asked her husband if the boy could move in with them. Her husband had been reluctant because the kid had gotten into trouble in the past and had even been suspended from school on several occasions. Still, he'd always been polite and helpful whenever he'd been on the Rocking C, and Teresa had suspected he'd only been acting out because of his sad childhood and difficult living situation.

Dave had begged them to let the boy stay with them, but his father had been firm in his decision. Teresa hadn't pushed her husband, although she always suspected she could have gotten him to see reason.

Shortly thereafter, the boy ran away from his foster home and was never heard from again. Dave had been inconsolable for nearly a year, and his relationship with his father had suffered terribly because of it.

Teresa had wished that she would have insisted that they take the boy in. And she'd always wondered what might have happened, how he might have fared if she had provided him a loving home. She also wondered if Dave and his father's relationship might have been a happier one, especially since her husband had died of a heart attack shortly after Dave joined the Marines in his one and only act of sheer rebellion.

To appease her guilt, Teresa had promised herself that, from then on, the Rocking C Ranch would always have its paddocks open for any stray, whether it had four legs or two.

And since Chloe had resolved to keep the ranch running exactly as Teresa would have done had she still been alive, that meant letting a hit-and-run victim who couldn't recall his own name recover there.

By the time she reached the medical center, it had grown dark outside and was threatening to rain. She turned into the hospital parking lot and pulled into a spot close to the entrance.

After entering the lobby, which had been decorated with twinkly lights and a big Christmas tree near the front window, she took the elevator to the third floor, where the nurses' station was a flurry of activity, reminding her of the shift changes at the Sheltering Arms. But thanks to the administrator at the nursing home who'd fired her rather than the incompetent nurse she'd reported, Chloe was no longer a part of the staff.

She checked out the room numbers until she spotted 327. The door was open, so she walked in. But she stopped short when she saw the wounded man standing near his bed, wearing a pair of tattered jeans, his broad chest bare.

Unable to help herself, she watched as he attempted to put on a torn black sweatshirt he must have been wearing at the time of the accident. His left hand was wrapped in an oversize bandage, and his muscled form struggled with the effort.

"Would you like... I mean, I could..."

He glanced over his shoulder, those amazing blue eyes locking in on hers and exposing something deep within, something vulnerable.

"Thanks, but I've got it." His handsome face bore a couple of scrapes, but other than that, he appeared strong and healthy. She could hardly tell that he'd been brought in on a gurney last night.

Maybe she should have taken a few extra minutes to freshen up and change out of her work clothes. Not that she was dirty or unkempt. It's just that he...well, she...

Oh, forget it. She didn't have time to let her thoughts drift into girlish, romantic notions.

"I don't mean to interfere if you'd rather do it your-self. It's just that, with the bandage and all, I thought..." She gave her head a little toss. "I'm sorry. I guess I shouldn't have just barged into your room like that. But...well, you're Joe Wilcox, right?"

"That's what they tell me." He pointed toward a stack of papers on the bed tray with his bandaged hand, yet her focus remained on his broad shoulders, on the scat-ter of dark chest hair that ran along taut abs and trailed into the waistband of his jeans.

"Do you remember me?" she asked.

"You're the woman who came in last night to iden-tify me. Chloe Dawson, right?"

She tossed him a smile. "Yes, that's me. I'm glad you remembered."

"Don't be too optimistic," he said. "I can recall ev-erything as far back as the ambulance ride. Anything before that is a giant black spot in my mind. Besides..." He patted the paperwork one more time. "Your name is on my discharge sheet."

"So Dr. Nielson told you that I was coming to pick you up?"

"Yep. Right before she signed off on my chart. I think she was eager to get home to her new baby. Not that I can blame her."

So he liked children? That ought to mean he was one of the white hats and that she had nothing to worry about by being alone with him.

"Do you have kids?" she asked.

He froze, and his blue eyes darted upward as if he had to look up the answer in his cranial database. "I have no idea. But that's not what I meant. I can't blame the doc for wanting to ditch this place as soon as she could. Hospitals give me the creeps."

Maybe, if she prodded him with enough questions, she'd latch on to the thread that would unravel all of his suppressed memories. "Have you been in the hospital before?"

"I don't know the answer to that, either. I'm going to guess that I have—and that I didn't like it."

"Why?"

"Because I can't wait to get out of here." He finally managed to slip on the sweatshirt. "You ready to go?"

"Sure. If you are."

He snatched a white plastic bag off the floor by his chair and headed out the door. As she tried to keep up with his determined pace, her dusty cowboy boots clicked along the polished corridor floor.

"Wait," she called out just before he reached the elevator. "I realize you're in a hurry to leave and would probably hitch a ride with the first ship setting sail, but Dr. Nielson is releasing you to my care. So let's slow down just a minute. Is there anything in that discharge paperwork that I need to know about before we hightail it out of here?"

"Sorry." He handed her the top sheet off his stack for her to read. "Listen, Miss Dawson."

When she looked up from the paper he'd given her and caught his gaze—or rather, when those amazing blue eyes caught hers—her tummy did a somersault.

He smiled. "It's *miss*, right?"

Was he asking if she was single? Or just trying to be polite?

While working at the Stagecoach Inn, she'd gotten used to men—old and young, drunk and sober—

hitting on her. And she was usually pretty quick on the draw when it came to letting them know she wasn't interested.

But she'd make an allowance for the sexy marine who was still probably disoriented from the accident and the shock of having his memory banks wiped clean—at least, temporarily.

"Yes, it is. But let's make that Chloe."

"All right," he said. "Thanks for picking me up, Chloe. And you might as well call me Joe, although, I may not answer to it."

Why? Had he realized that the sheriff might have mistaken him for someone else?

No, she'd been told that his photo and name lined up. "I suppose, if you don't remember who you are, your name wouldn't sound familiar."

"That's the problem. Something about that name doesn't feel right, although I have no idea why. Maybe because my brain is still so scrambled." He let out a weary sigh. "Anyway, you don't really have to be responsible for me. I waited for you to get here because Dr. Nielsen seems like a nice woman, and I don't want to get her in trouble with the hospital bigwigs. But you can just drop me off at a nearby homeless shelter or rescue mission. I'll be fine."

She couldn't possibly dump him just anywhere, especially in his condition. Yet he turned his back and continued on his way, his only goal the hospital exit.

"Joe," she called out.

At the sound of his name—or maybe just her voice—he turned in response.

With her boots still planted in the middle of the hall,

she asked, "Have you ever stayed in a homeless shelter or a rescue mission?"

"I don't know."

For a guy who didn't seem to know very much about himself, he had no problem putting one combat boot in front of the other and pretending that nothing was wrong.

"Have you ever been to Brighton Valley?" she asked.

"Don't know that, either."

She wondered if he was getting tired of sounding like a broken record. "We don't have any homeless shelters or rescue missions here. There's a community church that lets people sleep in the basement, but the pastor usually goes home before now, so I doubt that they're open."

"Then I appreciate your offer to give me a ride and a place to stay for a day or two—at least, until my memory returns."

"No problem. Dave and his family would have done the same."

The furrow in his brow deepened as if he was reaching deep into his memory banks, only to find them empty. Then he nodded and continued to the elevator.

She followed him. When the doors opened, they stepped inside.

His fingers lingered over the panel for longer than necessary, so she pressed the *L* for lobby. Again, she reminded herself that by taking him home she was doing the right thing. After all, she couldn't very well let him wander the streets if he couldn't even operate a simple elevator.

He glanced at her, and his blank stare tore at her heart. Had the gravity of his situation finally sunk in?

"You sure you don't mind me bunking with you?" he asked.

"Of course not. You're a friend of Dave's, and honestly, it's his ranch. I'm only doing what he and his mother would have done for any of their friends."

"I'll try to make it up to you—the inconvenience and what not—when I figure out who I am and what I'm good for."

"Judging by the dosage of painkillers Dr. Nielsen sent home with you, I don't think you'll be much good at anything for a few days. So let's get you well first." She nodded toward the main entrance to the lobby. "Come on, let's go."

He didn't need any convincing, soon taking the lead as they left the holiday-decorated lobby, leaving Bing Crosby crooning about dreams of a white Christmas behind.

Other than the soles of their boots tapping on the dusty concrete, they walked in silence until they reached the well-lit parking lot. Then Joe paused to look around.

Was he having a breakthrough?

"I'm not sure where we are," he said, "or what's nearby. But the doc told me to take the medicine when I eat. And for some weird reason, I have a real craving for Mexican food. Is there a taco shop nearby? Someplace where I can get some good *menudo* or *albondigas?*"

The way the Spanish words rolled off his tongue—as if he was a native speaker—surprised her. That was an interesting twist since Wilcox wasn't a typical Mexican surname.

Maybe he wasn't who they thought he was. That was a possible cause for alarm, but the USMC tattoo she'd seen before he'd put on that sweatshirt was enough to waylay at least some of her concern.

"Tía Juana's is a drive-through," she said. "And it's not too far from here. We can pick up something on the way back to the ranch."

"Thanks. That sounds great. And as a side note, I'd offer to pay, but you'll have to take my IOU. The sheriff was supposed to drop off my wallet at the hospital earlier today, but he hasn't done that yet."

"No problem," she said. "But as a side note of my own, I'm sorry."

"About what? Me not having any cash? That's the least of my problems."

"I know. And it must be horribly frustrating for you. I can't imagine what you're going through."

Fortunately, though, he'd just had a change in luck. Joe Wilcox now had Chloe Dawson to watch out for him—and with no one else to nurse these days, she intended to focus all her TLC on him.

By the time they reached the ranch, Joe was beyond exhausted. It had taken all his energy to finish off the spicy Mexican soup he'd ordered at Tía Juana's and to eat a couple bites of a quesadilla. Then he'd washed down his pills with a glass of iced tea.

"I'll show you to the guest room," Chloe said.

He followed her out of the kitchen, through a cozy living room with a stone fireplace and a built-in bookshelf, past a staircase leading to the second floor. He wondered where she slept. He knew better than to ask, though. No need for her to think he had ulterior motives, although she was one hell of a pretty woman.

He'd always been attracted to blondes…

Hadn't he? While that bit of information seemed to be a memory, it certainly wasn't one that was going to be very useful.

Still, Chloe's hair was a platinum shade that hung down her back in soft, shimmering waves he was tempted to touch and to watch slip through his fingers.

He kept his hands to himself, though. The last thing he wanted to do was to step out of bounds before he'd spent ten minutes alone with her. Besides, he wasn't up to fighting weight yet.

And speaking of hands... He glanced at the oversize bandage that was more trouble than it was worth. The tape was already flapping up. He'd told the nurse who'd put it on that he hadn't needed it, but she'd insisted, and he'd been too tired and rheumy to argue.

As he followed Chloe to the hall, she pointed out a bathroom on the left, then led him to the first door on the right. "I'd give you Dave's room, but if he shows up, he'll need a place to sleep. So this will have to do."

"I'd be happy on the couch. All I need is a pillow and blanket."

"We can do better than that," she said.

"'We'?" He hadn't realized that she might not live alone.

"Sorry. I'm actually just a guest here myself, so I don't consider the house mine." She flipped on the light switch, illuminating a small room with a double bed, a single nightstand and a dresser that rested near the window. "Would you like me to find you something to sleep in? There should be some men's pajamas in Dave's room."

Something told him he'd prefer to sleep in the raw,

but he decided not to mention that. "No, thanks. My boxers will have to do."

"Okay." She bit down on her bottom lip, as though worried about something.

"I plan on crashing the minute my head hits the pillow," he added. "I doubt I'll wake up until morning."

"Good." She brightened a moment, and then her smile slipped away. "I mean, a good night's sleep ought to do wonders."

An awkwardness settled around them, but Joe was too far gone to ponder why—or to even care.

"I'll leave you alone so you can get some rest," she said. "I'll see you in the morning."

"Thanks again."

"You're more than welcome." She waited a beat, as if still struggling with something. Attraction maybe?

Well, that was too damn bad. As nice as he might have found that before his accident, his jumbled and sleepy brain was too intent upon hitting the sheets— alone.

Of course, that didn't mean he'd feel the same way tomorrow.

For a guy who didn't know who or where he was, Joe had gotten a fairly good night's sleep. But now, as the morning rays lit the guest bedroom, he winced and stretched out his bum knee, hoping the ache would ease. He must have exasperated an old injury, because he'd spotted some nasty scarring earlier.

He had no idea what had happened to him. A normal, healthy guy who hadn't jarred his brains on the highway would have remembered how he'd messed himself up like that, especially since it looked as though he'd had surgery to correct it.

Damn. He hated not knowing anything about himself—who he was, where he was from, where he'd planned to go next.

At the sound of footsteps padding down the hall, he turned to the doorway, where the pretty blonde stood holding a stack of folded clothes.

"Good morning," she said. "How are you feeling?"

"Okay, I guess. Last night, before dozing off, I convinced myself that I would wake up feeling completely back to normal and with my memory intact."

"And…?"

"My head doesn't feel nearly as bad as before. But my memory?" He clucked his tongue. "Still nothing."

"How about a cup of coffee? Maybe a jolt of caffeine will trigger something."

Just seeing his pretty caretaker wearing a snug black sweater, leaning sexily in the doorway was enough to jolt him wide awake. But he wasn't about to make a comment like that. "Sure, coffee sounds great."

"How do you like it?"

"Black." The fact that he'd had an answer for her was enough to make him think his memory might actually return before long. He just wished it would hurry up. The brain fog was enough to make him climb the walls.

"You got it," she said. "How about bacon and eggs? I could also whip up some oatmeal or maybe some hot-cakes for you. Do you have a preference?"

Nothing jumped out at him. "I'll have whatever you're having."

"Nonfat Greek yogurt and bananas?"

No, he'd pass on the healthy crap. A slow grin tugged

at his lips. "Would hotcakes and bacon be too much trouble?"

She tossed him a sunny smile. "Not at all. Do you want me to serve you in here?"

While having a beautiful blonde sit on his bed, spoon-feeding him, triggered an intriguing vision and opened up some interesting possibilities, he didn't want her to think of him as an invalid. "No, I'll come out to the kitchen."

She lifted the folded clothing in her arms. "I brought you something you can wear—pants and shirts that belong to Dave. I also put fresh towels on the bathroom counter."

A shower sounded good. And so did having breakfast with her. "Thanks."

"Did you want to eat first?"

"If you don't mind. I want to take another dose of my pain medication, and I'm not supposed to do that on an empty stomach."

"You got it. I'll have it on the table in no time at all." She tossed him another smile, then placed the clothing on the top of the dresser.

When she turned and left the room, he threw off the covers, wincing when he bumped the scrape on his knuckles that was no longer protected by the bandage he'd removed, and got out of bed. He couldn't very well join her for breakfast without clothes. And since he was going to postpone the shower for later, he snatched the pair of folded jeans off the stack she'd set on top of the dresser, slipped them on and followed the aroma of sizzling bacon to the kitchen, where he found Chloe standing at the stove, her back to him. Her long blond hair had been pulled back into a ponytail.

Apparently, she hadn't heard him approach the kitchen, so he could just stand here and enjoy the view. But something told him not to get caught up in romantic dreams when he had no idea who he was or where he was going—or if there was a family waiting for him somewhere. So he decided to let his presence be known. "Something sure smells good."

At the sound of Joe's voice, Chloe turned to the kitchen doorway, where he stood wearing one of Dave's T-shirts and a pair of jeans. Yet that's where any similarities between the two men ended.

Dave had been fair-haired and on the thin side, while Joe was dark-haired with an olive complexion. His bulkier frame filled out that T-shirt in a way Dave never had.

"Is there anything I can do to help?" he asked.

"No, I have everything under control. Just come on in and have a seat."

As he complied, taking one of the kitchen chairs near the bay window that looked out into the nearest pasture, she poured him a mug of coffee and carried it to the table.

He thanked her, then took a sip. "You know, I really appreciate you providing me with a temporary place to stay, although I don't like the idea of causing you extra work."

"It's no problem."

"Maybe not, but I'd be happy to help out any way I can."

Since the ranch hand who usually helped Tomas with the chores had taken some time off to visit his family in Mexico, there was plenty to do. "That's nice of you to offer. And I might take you up on it—once you're feeling strong enough."

He smiled, revealing a pair of dimples and a glimmer in those amazing blue eyes. For a moment, she lost her train of thought.

"I'll start today," he said, "but don't worry. I'll take it slow and easy."

"Let's wait until tomorrow. I'd feel better if you had a little more time to rest."

"All right. Then I'll just have to hang out here at the house. But I promise not to get in your way or cause you any trouble."

Something told her that any trouble that came her way would be of her own making. "I'm sure you won't be. And to be honest with you, it'll be nice to have someone to talk to every now and then."

The big old ranch house could get lonely at times, especially in the evenings.

"So you're a guest here, too," he said.

She nodded, then turned back to the hotcakes that were browning on the griddle. She flipped each one over, then reached for a platter on which she could put them as soon as they were done.

"So what do you do when you're not nursing the injured?" he asked.

"I'm between jobs right now, which worked out okay in the long run. Tomas, the ranch foreman, is shorthanded, so I've been helping out when I can."

In truth, Tomas was a good worker—and he tried hard. But he'd never really had a supervisory role before. But when the previous foreman retired, Chloe had to find someone to step up to the plate. If she'd had more money to work with to offer a fair wage to someone better equipped, she would have. As it was, she promoted him based upon seniority.

"When you go back to job hunting," Joe said, "what kind of work do you do?"

"I used to be an aide at an assisted-living facility in town. I also plan to attend nursing school next semester."

"Pretty cool. I have my very own Florence Nightingale to help me get back on the mend."

She turned to face him again and smiled. "Nursing has always been a dream of mine."

Of course, after being terminated from the Sheltering Arms, she'd spent a little time wondering if she'd pinned her heart on the wrong dream.

Had Teresa Cummings, Dave's mother, still been alive, Chloe would have shared her disappointment and concern over her firing, which had seemed so unfair.

Then again, if Teresa had been alive, she would have advised Chloe to handle things differently at the time than she had, to confront her boss, to stir the pot. And if the administrator had seen fit to fire her anyway, Teresa might have encouraged her to file a wrongful termination suit.

But Chloe had never liked making waves. So she'd rolled over and walked away from the one job that had been the perfect fit for her.

She was tempted to share the details with Joe, but she bit her tongue. What did she really know about him?

Sure, she was drawn to him, although she blamed that on him being injured and her having a nurse's heart. She'd always been a nurturer, and she knew she'd make a good R.N. someday. But it wasn't just her heart Joe had touched. There was something about *him* she found attractive.

But she'd already had one bad relationship, if you could even call it that. Either way, she'd made a big mistake and didn't trust her judgment or instincts about men these days. And as long as she didn't act upon that attraction, they ought to get along just fine.

Chapter Three

By ten o'clock, Chloe had done two loads of laundry, cleaned the stove and washed the big bay window near the antique oak table. She enjoyed having her morning coffee where she could look out into the yard and pastures, so keeping the glass spotless had always been a priority.

While she worked, she kept the noise down. Joe might have offered to help her out on the ranch, but not long after eating breakfast and taking his pain medication, he'd mentioned being dizzy and had returned to the guest room and taken a nap. And she was glad that he'd done so.

Like it or not, he'd suffered a concussion. There was no way she would let him push himself too hard until he'd fully recovered.

She'd grown up as an army brat—the only girl with two older brothers, so she knew how stubborn men could be and how hard it was to admit their weakness. She'd keep that in mind the next time he offered to help. In the meantime, she continued to do her morning chores.

Next up was the kitchen floor. She'd just entered the mudroom to retrieve the plastic bucket and mop when the phone rang, so she hurried back to the kitchen and answered the old-style wall-mounted telephone before the noise disturbed Joe.

"Chloe," the caller said, "it's Betsy Nielson. How's our patient doing this morning?"

"He had a good breakfast. Now he's resting again."

"Good. Is he able to remember anything yet?"

"Not that I've seen so far."

"Give it some time. My husband, Jason, suffered from amnesia about four years ago. It was pretty tough on him, but his memories slowly began to return."

"How long did it take?"

"A couple of weeks. But each case is different, so it's impossible to predict. Just encourage Joe to be patient and let nature take its course."

"I will." Chloe wrapped the coiled phone cord around her index finger. "Has there been any news? I mean, how is the investigation going?"

"I haven't heard, but I'm sure Sheriff Hollister will be contacting Joe soon to give him an update."

"That's good. Joe will be eager to talk to him."

After the call ended, Chloe placed the receiver back in the cradle on the wall. She was eager to hear what the sheriff had to say, too. She hadn't heard from Dave in months and wondered where he was—and why he'd sent a letter to her through someone else.

A few weeks ago she'd written to him, but he hadn't responded. Then, just last Monday, she'd found her letter in the mailbox. The military had forwarded it to Dave, using the ranch address, which led her to believe his tour of duty had ended and that he'd been discharged.

If that was the case, then why hadn't he contacted her or come home yet? If he had actually been discharged, then he was no longer in Afghanistan. And that was a relief. Sure, his attachment to her had made her uncomfortable, but that didn't mean she didn't care about him.

She wasn't sure why he'd latched on to her like he had. She suspected that stress, battle fatigue and the recent death of his mother had all compounded and caused him to assume their friendship was something it had never been.

She'd done her best to explain that to him, but he couldn't seem to get the picture. Finally, when he began naming the children he'd imagined them having, she'd sent him a nice letter, trying to be kind, yet firm and direct.

Of course, she'd have to move off the ranch now that he was home. She couldn't risk having him think that there was any chance of her changing her mind about the two of them having a future together. Maybe, if he was out of the service and back in Brighton Valley, he could be more realistic about their relationship.

Either way, she would leave the Rocking C as soon as he arrived. She'd been looking after the ranch and trying to hold things together for him while he was gone, but her savings were just about gone, and the bills were still mounting up. She hoped he returned while he could still dig his way out of the hole he probably didn't know he was in.

"A penny for your thoughts."

Chloe turned to find Joe standing in the kitchen doorway. He was still wearing the same clothes. Even though he hadn't yet showered and appeared to be a bit battered, he looked as sexy as ever.

"My thoughts aren't worth much," she said, shaking off her worries and forcing a smile.

"Either way, I'm sorry, Chloe. I didn't mean to offer my services, then get dizzy and pass out on you."

Her smile deepened. "Don't give that a second thought. There'll be plenty to keep you busy when the time comes. It's best if you take it easy for now."

She couldn't help taking in his broad chest, the masculine bristle he'd yet to shave and those piercing blue eyes that seemed to see right through her. Again, she couldn't help comparing him to Dave, which wasn't fair to the other man. Not when Joe was drop-dead gorgeous.

He seemed to be checking her out just as closely as she'd been assessing him. Flushing, she tucked a strand of hair behind her ear, wishing she'd put on something other than jeans this morning.

At the sound of an approaching vehicle's engine, Chloe peered out the window and into the yard, where a police car pulled up.

"The sheriff is here," she said.

Joe stiffened. A flicker of emotion tumbled across his face, while apprehension marred his brow.

The poor man. Chloe crossed the room, reached out and touched his forearm, felt the warmth of his body heat. "It'll be okay."

His gaze seemed to say, *I hope you're right,* yet the tension in his stance suggested he had his doubts. Then he pulled free and headed for the living room, with her following behind.

Joe opened the front door, where a uniformed law enforcement officer stood on the stoop.

"I'm Shane Hollister," the sheriff said. "I'm heading up the investigation into your hit-and-run accident."

The words wadded up in Joe's throat. What was he supposed to say, other than "Thank God. What news do you have?"

Yet for some reason, facing the lawman sent a wisp of apprehension through him.

Damn. Did he have some reason to feel guilty?

Rather than stew about all the memories that evaded him, he shook off the uneasiness and said, "Hello, Sheriff."

Hollister gave him a once-over. "It's good to see you up and around. How are you doing?"

"Not bad. But I still can't remember squat—if that's what you mean."

"Well, maybe I can help." The sheriff handed him a wallet. "I meant to give you this before you left the hospital, but I missed you."

"That's okay." Joe turned the dark leather over in his hands, then flipped it open. He pulled out the California driver's license.

Sure enough, that was his photo staring back at him, verifying his name was Joseph Wilcox, even if it still didn't sound familiar. According to his address, he lived on base at Camp Pendleton.

"Please," Chloe told the sheriff, "come in and have a seat."

Hollister chose one of the chairs near the fireplace, then pulled a small notepad from his breast pocket. He flipped through a couple of pages before launching into his reason for coming by.

"We got a hit on your military service record," he told Joe. "It looks like you were medically discharged from the Marine Corps a few months ago."

If that were the case, then his address was no longer valid.

"The military won't release much of your information," Hollister said, "but I have a buddy up at the Houston NCIS office looking into it for me."

"NCIS?" Chloe asked.

"It stands for Naval Criminal Investigative Service," Hollister explained. "They work with both the navy and the Marine Corps, so my friend should be able to access info for us. Hopefully we'll know more later this week."

"Was there any word about Joe serving with Dave?" Chloe asked. "Or do you have any idea where Dave might be?"

"Not yet. That's something my contact at NCIS might be able to provide." Hollister turned his focus back to Joe. "It looks like you joined the Marines about six months after your eighteenth birthday. You were a staff sergeant at the time of your discharge, which tells me that you probably had a stellar service record to move up the ranks so quickly."

Joe blew out a ragged sigh. "That's good to know, I suppose. It's too bad I can't recall some of that stellar service myself."

Chloe eased up to his chair and placed her hand on his shoulder. "Dr. Nielson said to give it some time. Her husband suffered from amnesia a few years back, and his memory returned slowly over the course of a few weeks."

"That sounds like ages to me," Joe said. "I've never had much patience."

"You haven't?" As if eager to grab on to anything positive, Chloe gave his shoulder a gentle squeeze. "I'd say that's good news."

Joe looked up at her and furrowed his brow. "What do you mean?"

"If you know that so readily about yourself, then it sounds like a memory has returned already."

Unfortunately, Joe didn't find that very helpful and returned his gaze to the sheriff. "Have you found out anything else about the person who hit me?"

"Judging from the tire tracks and a couple of eyewitness accounts, we think the perp was parked at the Stagecoach Inn and jumped the curb before hitting you. I have a couple of my deputies questioning all the patrons who were there that night—and looking over their cars to see if there's any corresponding bodywork damage. But that's assuming it was one of the locals. We're still gathering credit-card records in case it was someone who was just passing through on the highway and decided to stop off at the bar for a few drinks to wait out the evening traffic."

"I appreciate your efforts to find whoever it was who hit me," Joe said. "And for helping me piece my life back together."

"No problem." The sheriff put away his notepad and got to his feet. "That's my job. But you might want to consider that this wasn't a mere accident."

Chloe's hand slipped off Joe's shoulder. "Why do you say that?"

"There weren't any skid marks, so either the driver didn't see you or was aiming right at you."

The thought that someone might have been out to get him didn't sit well, but when Joe shot a glance at Chloe and saw the worry that marred her brow, his concern shifted.

He didn't like seeing her on edge, which was surely the case since she'd removed the warmth of her support when she'd taken her hand from his shoulder. Neither did he want to bring any trouble her way. But he wasn't about to reassure her with false promises, especially if he had no clue what kind of complications his presence could cause.

"I don't want to alarm you or be a conspiracy theorist," the sheriff added, "but there's a lot we still don't know about you. And with your temporary memory loss, you can't answer any of those questions for us. I can't ignore the fact that someone might have been out to hit you for some reason. Or that they might not want you in town."

Joe wished he could reassure both Chloe and the sheriff, but he couldn't. He might not feel like a wanted man, but how would he know for sure? The lawman was probably just trying to cover all the bases, which was wise. It made sense not to restrict his investigation to the easiest, most obvious case solution.

And while Joe had hoped that the sheriff's arrival would toss him a life raft of sorts, instead, it had only opened up more worries, more concerns, more what-ifs.

What little solid ground he'd once felt under his feet had been whisked away, leaving him alone, tossed about on a choppy sea with no compass, no oars and no sign of the shore.

"So what do we do?" Chloe asked.

We? He couldn't expect her to help. She'd done a lot already. But the thought of having someone in his corner of the rowboat helped a little.

"My suggestion would be for Mr. Wilcox to try to

keep a low profile," Hollister said. "It might be best if he stayed here at the ranch until we can investigate further."

"I'd hoped someone in town might recognize him and be able to tell us more about who he is—and why he's here," Chloe said.

Joe wasn't as concerned for his own safety as he was for hers. So far, she'd been a friend, an ally in his messed-up world, and he didn't want to do anything that might put her in jeopardy.

"Maybe it's best if I moved on," he said.

Chloe placed her hand back on his shoulder. And this time, her fingertips sent a whisper of heat through his veins. Her gaze met his, stirring something deep within. "Where would you go?"

He raked a hand through his hair. How the hell did he know? But he'd figure something out. He had to, before this beautiful stranger turned his mixed-up brain even more inside out.

"It has to be frustrating not to know who you are or why you're here," the sheriff said. "But from a safety standpoint, I think it's more important to get to the bottom of this accident first and then figure out the memory problem later."

Joe could see how Hollister would be more concerned with a crime being committed in his quaint small town. And while it was helpful of the sheriff to go above the call of duty and look for his personal records, it wasn't as if Joe was suffering from a simple little "memory problem." It was a full-blown loss of identity, a loss of control over his life. And his gut clenched at the thought, at the possibilities....

What if he had somewhere else to be at this exact second? Or what if someone needed him, but he was AWOL?

Crap. What if the person waiting for him was his wife?

"Uh, Sheriff," he said. "Do you know if my military file mentioned anything about me being married or having kids?"

"It didn't say specifically, but you don't have any military dependents listed. So my guess would be that you're single."

Joe released a pent-up sigh. At least he didn't have a family worrying about him. Not that he was completely off the hook. There could be someone else who needed him, someone who…

No, that wasn't true. He wasn't sure how he knew that there was no one else, that no one had ever worried about him. He just did.

"All right," Chloe said. "I'll keep Mr. Wilcox on the ranch while you finish looking into whoever did this."

"Sounds good." The sheriff made his way to the door, then turned and looked at Joe. "I'll keep you posted as to what else we uncover. And I'll call the minute I hear anything from the military."

"Thanks. I'd appreciate that." Joe supposed he should feel better, yet his jumbled mind couldn't wrap itself around so many possibilities. And that left him just as confused as he'd been the moment he'd woken up in the E.R.

Well, almost as confused.

"I'll walk you outside," Chloe told the sheriff.

As the two stepped onto the porch and continued toward the police car, Joe remained in the living room, feeling like a kid left behind so the grown-ups could have a discussion in private.

But he could see why Chloe might want to talk to the cop in private. No doubt she wanted to relay her fears and misgivings about living with a random stranger.

Hell, if she was afraid, he'd have to leave—no matter what Hollister had suggested. Too bad he had no idea where to go.

For the time being, he headed back to the kitchen, determined to mop the floor and to finish the chore Chloe had started before Hollister had arrived. He figured that he might as well make himself helpful around the house and the ranch so she wouldn't think of him as an obligation or a burden.

Okay. So he was also curious about what was going on outside, what was being said.

He placed the bucket into the sink, then turned on the faucet. While the water flowed out of the spigot, he looked out the big kitchen window, where Hollister and Chloe stood near the squad car.

The sheriff opened the driver's door and reached across the seat. Then he handed an envelope to Chloe.

Was that Dave's letter?

For just being a "family friend," she was certainly concerned about the guy. Not that Joe had any claim to his personal Florence Nightingale, but he couldn't stop the uneasy feeling rolling through his stomach.

Or the prickle of jealousy that sketched over him, urging him to try and make Chloe experience her own case of amnesia and forget whatever it was that she felt for Dave Cummings.

Chloe recognized Dave's loopy penmanship the moment Sheriff Hollister handed over the letter. She'd been tempted to tear into it right then and there, but she merely stared at the worn and smudged envelope that someone had folded in half, measuring the weight of it in her hand.

Apparently someone had been carrying it around for a while—either Dave or Joe. Maybe even both of them.

"I'm curious about the contents of that letter," the sheriff said.

She could understand why, but she was reluctant to read what Dave had to say in front of anyone. She wasn't sure what he'd written—or how it would make her feel. She'd never liked hurting anyone's feelings or angering them, and realizing that she'd either hurt or angered Dave didn't sit well with her.

"There might be something inside that would suggest why Wilcox is here," Sheriff Hollister added.

"I thought you would have opened it as part of your investigation," Chloe said.

"It's a sealed envelope. I can't read it without a warrant, and since Dave Cummings wrote it to you, there's no reason for me to request one." Sheriff Hollister reached into his pocket and pulled out a business card. "If you find any clues that might help with my investigation, I'd appreciate it if you'd let me know."

"Of course."

He nodded, then climbed into his squad car. "Everything I've learned about Wilcox suggests that he's law-abiding. But if you have reason to believe otherwise, give me a call."

"I will. Thank you." She refolded the envelope, then shoved it into the back pocket of her jeans.

Rather than return to the house, she waited until the sheriff left and watched the black-and-white vehicle head down the drive, biding her time and tamping down her compulsion to tear into the missive.

While tempted to dash upstairs and pore over the contents so she could get an idea where Dave was and why Joe had possession of the letter in the first place, she reined in her curiosity. She'd already left Joe alone in the house long enough and didn't want him to think she was rude—or worse, suspicious of him. So she walked up the porch steps and entered the living room.

She thought her houseguest might have gone back to bed—and if he had, she wouldn't have blamed him. Those head injuries could really take a lot out of a person. But when she heard noise coming from the kitchen, she went looking for him there. She wouldn't have been surprised to see him fixing himself a snack. But she hadn't expected to find a bucket on the wet floor and to see him wringing out the mop.

"What are you doing?" she asked.

His movements stilled, and he leaned against the wooden handle, the muscles in his forearms flexed and primed for heartier work. "Thought I'd better help out and pay for my keep."

"You don't need to do that."

"Yes, I do. I don't like taking handouts." His eye twitched, and his brow furrowed, his words drifting off. Had a memory crossed his mind?

She was afraid to ask since she'd already jumped to that conclusion a couple of times, and she'd been wrong.

"At least, I don't think I do," he added.

"Dr. Nielson said that you should take it easy."

"Yeah, and she also told me to be patient, but something tells me I'm not one to sit around and wait for things to happen."

She continued to stand in the doorway, the letter burning a hole in her back pocket.

"I'll tell you what," Joe said. "I'm almost finished here. As soon as I dump out the dirty water, I'll go to the barn and check out the stables. That way, you can read the letter the sheriff gave you in private."

Chloe smoothed her hand over the front of her jeans, fingering the hemmed edge of the pocket, making sure it was still hidden inside. Had she been that obvious?

"I saw Hollister give it to you outside, and if I were in your boots, I'd be dying to read it, too. Especially if it says Joe Wilcox is a nutcase and you shouldn't let him within a hundred feet of you." He smiled, but she knew he was itching for a clue as to why he was here.

Still, she wanted to be alone when she read whatever Dave hadn't wanted to tell her in person.

If truth be told, she felt badly about possibly hurting his feelings while he was in a war zone, no matter how gentle she'd tried to be. And she regretted the distance her honesty had created between them.

"Thanks for understanding," she said. "I'll let you know if it says anything about you."

Joe nodded. Then he began to mop the floor under the table, which was the only dry spot left. After he finished, he leaned the mop against the wall and carried the bucket through the mudroom and out into the yard.

When Chloe was finally alone, she went into the living room, took a seat in the chair in which Sheriff Hollister had once sat and took the envelope from her pocket. After opening it, she withdrew the letter and unfolded the single sheet of paper.

Chloe,

If you're reading this letter, then that means Joe
found you for me and hand-delivered it.

   I can never thank you enough for what you did
for my mom during her last days, and I'm sorry
that my love and gratitude made you uncomfortable. Even though my feelings weren't recipro-
cated, that doesn't mean that I felt them any less.

   I can't think of anywhere else I'd rather be than
with you. But if you're not interested in what we
could have together, then I won't bother you again.
Goodbye.

Dave

Chloe read the short note several times, focusing
on the last cryptic part. Dave had a penchant for the
melodramatic, so it was hard to know what he meant.
Still, he didn't have to stay away. The ranch belonged
to him, and she would gladly turn the reins back over
to him when he came home.

If he came home. Joe clearly knew where he could
be found—that is, if his memory ever returned. When
it did, she'd ask him to contact Dave and tell him she
was leaving, that she couldn't stay on the Rocking C
forever.

But why hadn't Dave contacted her in person? And
why had he wanted the letter delivered when it would
have been much easier to mail it? Or even to call?

Had Dave asked Joe to evict her? Maybe, once she'd
cleared out of the house, Joe was to inform Dave so
that he could return to the Rocking C without having
to see her.

But if that was the case, all he'd had to do was say the word and she'd start packing.

However, she wouldn't leave the ranch unattended until he actually arrived. So he'd just have to man up and deal with her temporary presence.

In the meantime, what in the world was she going to do with Joe?

And what would he tell her once his memory returned? She had no idea.

For a moment, she pondered showing him Dave's letter, thinking it might jar his memory. But she didn't consider that option very long. She'd just tell Joe that Dave had asked him to deliver it in person.

Perhaps just her reassurance that Joe was actually Dave's friend was enough. It would have to be—until she figured out just what Dave meant when he said, "But if you're not interested in what we could have together, then I won't bother you again. Goodbye. Dave."

What if he'd actually been saying goodbye forever? What if Dave had…?

Oh, God. And what if, somehow, it had been her fault?

Chapter Four

As Joe made his way through the Rocking C barn, the smell of straw and dust stirred more than his senses. He stopped for a moment, scanning the walls where the tack hung and pondering the feeling of déjà vu that settled over him.

Had he actually been here before? It seemed as though he had.

Or was it something about the ranch or the scent of feed and leather that made him feel at home?

A horse whinnied, and he continued to walk to the back of the barn, where an Appaloosa was stabled.

"Hey there," he told the mare. "How's it going?"

She snorted, threw back her head, then stepped closer.

He reached in to stroke her neck. He didn't know how long he stood there, talking to the horse, striking up a friendship of sorts. Certainly long enough for Chloe to have read her letter from Dave.

He supposed he could go back into the house now, but he lingered in the barn, trying to wrap his mind around the cloak of familiarity. Too bad he wasn't having much luck.

Behind him, boot steps sounded. He glanced over

his shoulder and spotted the approach of a stocky, middle-aged cowboy.

When their eyes met, the man introduced himself. "I'm Tomas Hernandez, the ranch foreman. You must be Joe Wilcox."

For some reason, even though he'd been assured that his identity had been confirmed, the name still didn't seem to fit. That was probably to be expected with amnesia.

Shaking off the lingering uneasiness, Joe turned away from the horse and reached out a hand to greet the foreman.

"It's good to see you out and about," Hernandez said. "I heard about the accident. Sounds like you were lucky."

Joe didn't feel so lucky. He felt lost and out of control. But he wasn't about to whine about it. "I suppose it could have been a whole lot worse."

Hernandez nodded. "You're right. You still could be laid up in the hospital."

Or in the morgue.

Again, Joe let the reality of the thought pass. "The doctor said to take it easy, but I'm going stir-crazy. I never have been able to sit still."

He wasn't sure how he knew that. Maybe because he was chomping at the bit to get back to normal, whatever that might be.

"If you have any work that needs to be done," Joe added, "just say the word. I'd like to help out any way I can."

"Chloe said you're still recovering and won't be available for a while."

So they'd talked about him. Joe couldn't blame

them, he supposed. But he didn't like the idea of being a burden—or someone's problem. In fact, his gut twisted at the thought, and a shadow of uneasiness draped over him once more, this time weighing him down even worse than the amnesia did.

"I figure I'll take it easy today," he told Hernandez. "But I'll be ready to pitch in tomorrow."

"That's good to hear. I'm down a ranch hand, so there's plenty to keep us both busy for a while."

As the silence stretched between them, they assessed each other like two stray dogs wondering if they should be friends or foes.

Joe nodded toward the mare. "She's a pretty horse."

"Yes, she is. And she has good bloodlines, too. Her name's Lola. She's going to foal soon, so I brought her in and stabled her until her time comes."

Joe still couldn't shake the feeling that he'd been on the ranch before. And in the barn. Did Hernandez recognize him?

"Have you worked here long?" he asked the foreman.

"About four years." Hernandez lifted his hat, revealing a balding head. "It'll be five this coming February."

"I don't suppose you recognize me," Joe said.

"No, I'm afraid not."

"I thought maybe Dave had brought me around," he told the foreman.

"Not that I'm aware of."

That shot down his theory, he supposed. Maybe he'd grown up on a ranch. But where?

He scanned the barn again. So why did he have this feeling of déjà vu? Was his scattered brain playing tricks on him? Maybe. Still, Hernandez wasn't very forthcoming.

"When did Dave join the Marines?" he asked the foreman.

"About two and a half years ago. He and his father had a big falling out over something or other. And Dave enlisted to spite him."

"What'd they fight about?"

"Almost everything. But that last time was the worst. And I'm sure Dave was sorry about it afterward."

"You mean joining the corps?"

"Leaving home, mostly. His father died of a heart attack shortly after Dave finished recruit training. And I think Dave blamed himself for it. Last time he was here, to attend his mother's funeral, he told me he'd be home soon and wouldn't ever leave again. He asked me to look out for things until he did. But he hasn't contacted any of us in quite a while."

No wonder Chloe was eager to read that letter.

And now Joe was even more curious than ever to know what it said. He and Dave might be buddies, but they hadn't enlisted at the same time. According to what the sheriff had said, Joe had joined five years earlier.

He stroked his chin, felt the stubble of the beard he hadn't shaved this morning. That shower he'd been meaning to take after he'd taken his morning pain meds was long overdue.

"Well," he said to Hernandez, "I'm going to head back to the house. If you start making a list of chores you'd like me to do, I'll get started on them tomorrow."

"All right. I'll do that."

Joe gave Lola's neck one last stroke, then strode toward the barn door. He hated not knowing anything about himself. And while he continued to get some fleeting thoughts about his character and things he liked or disliked, he had no idea how to cobble them together.

After entering the living room, he took a moment to survey the leather furnishings, the built-in bookshelf in the far wall, the stone fireplace with photos lining the mantel. When he noticed one of a smiling marine in uniform, he made his way to the hearth so he could take a better look.

He lifted the brass frame and studied the fair-haired man's image. He wished he could say that he recognized him, but he didn't.

"That's Dave," Chloe said.

Joe turned toward her voice. She stood in the doorway that led down the hall to the bedrooms. The moment their gazes met, he felt another stirring—one that was far more appealing than the scent of leather and hay that had provoked his senses in the barn.

"His mother never understood why he'd joined the service in the first place," Chloe said. "As the only child, the only son, he knew his father expected him to stay on the ranch and take over someday. But I've sensed there was more to it than that. I think he had a blowup with his dad, although he never said anything to me about it."

Joe took another gander at the photo in his hand.

"Does he look familiar?" Chloe asked.

"No, I'm afraid not." Joe returned the frame to the mantel.

"Well, you definitely knew him. In his letter, he mentioned that he'd given it to you and asked you to bring it to me."

"That's all he had to say?"

She bit down on her bottom lip, as though struggling with the answer. "About you? Yes, that's all."

What else had Dave written? The rest of his message had obviously been personal and something she wasn't eager to share.

Joe figured he didn't have a right to ask if he could read it himself, although his curiosity was mounting. And so was his interest in what made Chloe tick, an interest that threatened to turn into full-blown attraction if he'd let it.

And maybe it was morphing into that anyway.

Even today, with her white-blond hair pulled into a ponytail that hung down her back and no makeup other than the pink lipstick she had nearly worn off, he found her intriguing.

She wasn't wearing anything fancy—just faded jeans and a blue, lightweight sweater. Yet she couldn't hide her wholesome beauty behind a plain Jane facade. Not when those whiskey-colored eyes had zeroed in on him and set his libido on end.

As if unaware of his thoughts, she crossed the room, joined him near the fireplace and reached for the framed photograph he'd just replaced on the mantel. As she stood within touching distance, her faint, lemon-blossom scent aroused more than his interest.

She studied the marine in the photo for a moment. While she did so, Joe studied her—the thick dark lashes, the delicate features of her face, the fullness of her lips...

"After Dave joined the service and his father passed away, his mom was left to run the ranch on her own." Chloe took one last look at the photo, then returned the frame to its rightful place on the mantel. "When she got sick, I tried my best to help in any way I could, but I didn't know anything about working on a ranch—although I'm learning."

"So you'll wait here until Dave returns home?"

She bit down on her lip again, then gave a slight shrug of her left shoulder. "Since Teresa had provided a home for me when I needed one, I felt a certain obligation to her. So I promised her I'd stay until then."

Did she feel obligated to Teresa's son, as well?

Again, Joe shook off the curiosity that plagued him. Well, at least he tried to. There was a lot Chloe had left unsaid, a lot he wanted to know about her. And since his past wasn't readily available to him, he focused on learning more about hers.

"So where are you from?" he asked.

She smiled wistfully. "Here, there and everywhere."

He leaned against the mantel, crossed his arms and tossed her a grin to soften his line of questioning. "So you don't like to be tied down to one place?"

"No, it's not that at all. My parents are both in the military, so we moved around a lot when I was a kid. I also had to change schools more often than seemed fair. So now that I'm on my own, I want to settle down and create some stability in my life."

Since she'd mentioned that Mrs. Cummings had taken her in when she'd needed a place to stay, he suspected she'd had a few bad breaks—or trouble at home.

"Do you see your family very often?" he asked.

"I used to try and spend the bigger holidays with them, but I wasn't able to do that last Christmas because they were stationed in Hawaii. And it looks like I'll be staying in Brighton Valley again this year, too."

He had a feeling that she wasn't happy about it, so he said, "That's too bad."

"Do you…" She paused, and her cheeks turned a rosy hue. "I'm sorry. I was going to ask about your family and their holiday traditions."

He shrugged a single shoulder. "Don't worry about it. I wish I had an answer for you."

Chloe reached out and touched his arm, sending a pulsing shot of heat through his veins. He glanced down at the delicate fingers that rested on his sleeve and warmed him from the inside out.

She wasn't wearing any jewelry. But what about her other hand?

He fought the compulsion to check out her left ring finger—something he'd neglected to do earlier. But he didn't want her to catch him in the act. So he looked into her eyes instead, nearly losing himself in her intoxicating gaze.

"Christmas always makes me homesick," she said. "My mother really does things up big. Probably to make me and my brothers feel as though we had a real home and more stability in our lives. But I'm stuck here this year. And apparently, you are, too. So we'll just have to roll with that and create a down-home, country-style Christmas for the two of us. That way, maybe we can help each other make a brand-new memory."

Her suggestion caught him off guard, although he wasn't sure why. The fact that his brain was still healing, maybe. And that she'd removed her hand from his arm, stealing the warmth of her touch.

But as she continued to peer into his eyes, to search his expression, to silently plead her case, he gave in. "Sure. Why not?"

He'd been tempted to shake off her offer for more reasons than one. But as he thought about it, he realized that he actually liked the idea of making new memories with Chloe.

When the buzzer on the dryer sounded, Chloe retrieved the last load of laundry. After folding the small batch of towels and linens, she carried them down the hall to put them away.

Before placing them in the linen closet, she decided to make a quick check of the guest bathroom to make sure there were plenty of clean washcloths for Joe to use.

She reached for the doorknob and gave it a turn. The locking mechanism made a click-click sound, but the door swung right open, releasing a bit of steam.

And revealing Joe standing at the counter, his face lathered with shaving cream, his body bare other than a small white towel wrapped around his waist.

Her cheeks warmed. "Oh, my gosh. I'm so sorry. I—"

"It's okay. I'm practically dressed."

No, it wasn't all right. And he was naked underneath that towel. All it would take was one simple little tug at the waist…

Reining in her sexual thoughts, she gathered her wits. "The door. You didn't lock it."

"Actually, I did. But apparently it isn't working."

Yeah, well… She supposed she could cast the blame on the lock—or on everyone else, including the man in the moon, but that didn't cool her cheeks. Nor did it hide the handsome man who was a sight to behold.

She swallowed—hard. It was nearly impossible to

think, let alone speak, so she nodded, turned and shut the door.

As she put away the folded washcloths into the linen closet, she fought the urge to slip outside and find some chores to do in the yard so she wouldn't have to return to the house. But that wasn't feasible. She'd have to go back inside eventually. So she may as well deal with the embarrassment.

Still, just living with Joe here, knowing that he was sleeping down the hall, just two doors away from her bedroom, sent her thoughts scampering in an unexpected direction.

She blew out a ragged sigh. The flash of physical attraction she'd initially felt had magnified and left her feeling awkward and uneasy.

After placing the washcloths on the shelf where they belonged, she returned to the kitchen. It would be lunchtime soon, so she might as well whip up something to eat. She wondered if he'd like a tuna-salad sandwich.

She pulled the can opener from the drawer, a small mixing bowl from the cupboard, and mayonnaise, pickles and celery from the fridge. Then she searched the pantry for a can of tuna. She'd no more than shut the door when Joe said, "The bathroom is free now."

If she could have gotten away with pretending she hadn't heard him, she would have done it. As it was, she slowly turned to face him, her cheeks warming all over again.

She glanced down at her feet, willing herself to cool. When she looked back to his freshly shaven face and those striking blue eyes, her breath caught, her heart thumped and her cheeks warmed all over again.

"I'm sorry about walking in on you," she said. "I should have realized that you might have been in there."

"Like I said, it wasn't a big deal. I was covered up."

Yes, but just barely.

Fortunately, he was dressed now, although in Dave's clothing. The pants were at least an inch too short, and the T-shirt, which stretched across his broad chest, didn't hide the rippling muscles underneath.

"I promise to knock next time," she said.

Joe chuckled. "And I'll put 'Repair the Bathroom Lock' at the top of my to-do list."

"Good idea." She offered him an appreciative smile, then turned her back and continued her search for the canned tuna.

Now that she'd seen the handsome marine in the buff—or pretty close to it—fixing that door lock would only solve half her problem because the image of him wearing only a smile and a skimpy towel was engrained in her mind.

And that was one breath-stealing memory she wasn't likely to forget any time soon.

Joe couldn't help enjoying Chloe's obvious discomfort. In fact, ever since she'd walked in on him shaving—and up until the time they sat down to eat lunch—she seemed to avoid making eye contact with him.

A couple of times, he'd been tempted to tease her, but he decided to let it go. No need to stir up those kinds of sexual thoughts when he wasn't in any position to do anything about them.

As Chloe stood from her seat at the kitchen table and

picked up their empty plates, she asked, "Do you need anything in town?"

Some clothing that actually fit him would be nice. But since he didn't want to ask any more of her than he had already, he said, "I can't think of anything. Why?"

"I'm going to visit a friend who's living in a nursing home near the Brighton Valley Medical Center. Afterward I'm going to stop at the market and run a few errands. I thought, since the sheriff didn't want you to go into town that I could pick up anything you might need."

"I can make do with whatever is here." He just hoped that he and Dave actually were friends. If not, and the guy came home to find Joe staying in his house, wearing his clothes and using his shaving kit, things could become awkward.

"All right," she said. "I won't be gone too long. And when I get back, I'll fix dinner."

"Is there anything I can do for you while you're gone?"

"If you happen to see Tomas, will you ask him to bring in the plastic storage boxes filled with Christmas decorations? I think Teresa kept them in the hayloft."

"I can get them for you."

"No, I'd rather you took it easy and rested today. Believe me, there's still going to be plenty for you to do once you're feeling better."

"I feel better already."

"Is that right?" She crossed her arms and tossed him an impish grin. "Then why are you still taking that pain medication?"

"Okay. So I'm not quite back to fighting weight. But I'm definitely better."

"I have no doubt about that. Still, I'd rather have

Tomas bring in the decorations when he has time. I'll save you for bigger, more important things."

"Like what?"

She flushed again, and this time he couldn't resist teasing her. "What's the problem?"

"Excuse me?"

"Your cheeks are red, and you keep looking at everything except me. Are you that bothered about walking in on me in the bathroom?"

"You're wrong. It didn't faze me a bit."

He didn't believe her. In fact, he suspected she was still reeling from having seen him half-dressed. And since she seemed to be so flustered by it, he found it a bit flattering. But he didn't want her to feel awkward about it.

"Don't be embarrassed," he said. "Those things happen."

"I'm not." She stood a little taller and lifted her chin. "It's a hazard of being blonde and fair. I flush easily— and usually for no reason whatsoever. It's really no big deal."

"Good. I'm glad to hear that."

She might claim to be immune to him, but he wasn't buying it. Still, it was nice to know that her body easily displayed the effects of heating up.

Without any conscious effort on his part, a vision came to mind—her curvy, fair-skinned body stretched out on his bed sheets, pink and rosy from his caresses, her hair splayed on his pillow, her eyes glazed with passion.

"So," she said, her voice interrupting his erotic daydream, "since you don't need anything, I'll take off and run my own errands. Try and get some rest while I'm gone."

He'd try, but he doubted he'd get much rest at all, especially if he was plagued with any more sexy visions of her. But on top of that, he also had something that would keep him busy for a while.

"By the way," he said, "I noticed a computer in the den. Would it be okay if I used it while you were gone?"

Her movements stilled, and her eyes grew wide. "Do you remember how?"

Judging by the way his thoughts had veered off course a few seconds ago, he also remembered how to make love to a beautiful woman. But there was no point in making Chloe any more uncomfortable than she already was.

"I still have all my same abilities," he said. "The only thing I've forgotten is the past."

"What do you plan to use the computer for?"

Something told him that he was a man who kept his thoughts and tactics close to the vest. But Chloe didn't appear to be suspicious, just curious. So he would let her in on his plan. "I'm going to search for clues about who I really am—not that I even know the first place to start looking."

"Good idea. I'll get you logged in. Then, when I come home, maybe you can share some new information with me."

Sure, he thought. *I'll share with you, just as soon as you share that letter with me.* But he smiled and kept that thought to himself.

He followed her to the den, where she set him up on an old desktop device that looked as though it was about to give up the ghost. Joe had no reason to suspect that he was any big computer whiz, but he could easily see that the PC was out-of-date. He couldn't recall having any expertise in technology or electronics, but he'd seen the fancy Geekon laptops that the nursing staff had used at the medical center.

There'd been something about the brand name that had struck a chord and triggered a feeling of familiarity. But he hadn't said anything to anyone about that. Why get excited about something he still couldn't put his finger on?

When his sexy Florence Nightingale was satisfied that he could operate the machine and that he wouldn't stay on it for more than an hour before giving his mind and body another rest, she left him alone in the den to search for clues he didn't know how to find.

Outside, the engine of the old ranch pickup started up, letting him know he was on his own for a while. So he typed in his name, only to get eighty-two thousand hits. So he narrowed his search.

Okay, apparently he was somewhat computer literate. But even that tidbit of information didn't tell him squat. And even an hour later, he still hadn't found anything to go on. He suspected that he'd be out of luck until his brain sorted itself out—or until the sheriff came by with more information.

But he wasn't going to give up that easily. So he typed in Dave Cummings, Brighton Valley and the Rocking C Ranch. This time, the search yielded a better result.

He found an article about the Brighton Valley High School music club and spotted a black-and-white photo of Dave and several of his bandmates.

As he continued his search, he uncovered obituaries for both Mr. Cummings and his wife. As he read them, a heaviness filled his chest, but he'd be damned if he knew why. The fact that they'd died fairly young, he supposed.

He found quite a few articles about Brighton Valley, and so he spent the next fifteen minutes reading through the city's online newspaper in the hope that something about the small Texas town would jump out at him.

The only article that came close to triggering any sense of significance was a fairly recent one about Clay Jenkins, the founder of Geekon Enterprises and mastermind behind creating its computers and repair stores. Jenkins had gone to school in nearby Wexler, but apparently Brighton Valley had claimed him as a native son.

The brains behind all the impressive Geekon products had recently moved back to town and had married a woman who'd been working in the local Zorba the Geek computer repair shop.

As Joe studied the picture of the billionaire, another sense of familiarity settled over him.

Why was that? Did he know the man? They appeared to be close in age.

After looking up more information on the big shot in the software industry, Joe decided that Clay's popularity and fame led to what little recognition he'd sensed.

He glanced at the small antique brass clock on one of the bookshelves. It was getting close to three o'clock, well after the hour when he'd promised to shut down the computer and take an afternoon nap. But he wanted to run one more search.

So he typed in Chloe Dawson. It wasn't the most common name, but it still garnered several hits. She'd said she was an army brat and had moved around a lot, so Joe wasn't really sure where her hometown of record would be. But a picture of a homecoming queen at a small school just outside of Fort Hood, Texas, certainly resembled the lovely woman who'd volunteered to nurse a poor, unknown former marine back to health.

She stood next to a handsome jock wearing a crown and a sash over his football uniform. Like her, he was holding a bouquet of roses and flashing a happy smile.

Chloe had been a pretty teenager who'd blossomed into a stunning beauty—even when she'd traded in the fancy gown for a pair of faded jeans and a flannel shirt.

That's why Joe had a difficult time wrapping his head around the possibility that a popular homecoming queen could be attracted to a short, scrawny band geek like Dave. Of course, Dave must have grown up and filled out after joining the Marines. But still, something didn't compute.

Maybe the two weren't involved in any sort of intimate relationship. Chloe had said they were only friends. But if that were the case, then why would she stay here on the ranch, breaking her back to keep things running for a guy who couldn't even find time to call or otherwise check in?

It seemed like a waste, especially when her heart and talents should be pursuing her desired career in the nursing field.

Another question continued to nag him. Why would Dave task a buddy with a mission to hand deliver a letter to the beautiful Miss Dawson when a phone call or a certified letter could have done the same job—and been a whole lot easier?

The delivery method he'd chosen meant the message had to be personal. And as much as Joe would like to get his hands on that letter to find out what was so important that he'd come to Brighton Valley in the first place, he'd sure hate to find out that he was lusting after his buddy's girl.

Chapter Five

The Sheltering Arms Nursing Home was located just two blocks down from the Brighton Valley Medical Center and next door to a senior apartment complex that also offered assisted living for the residents who needed additional care.

On the outside, the two-story brick building didn't look much different from any of the other medical offices that had sprung up around the hospital. But on the inside, the staff and volunteers did their best to provide a warm, cozy environment so the patients would feel more at home.

That was one of the things Chloe liked about the place. Most of the staff cared about the elderly residents and went above and beyond when it came to their comfort and care. The other thing was the seniors themselves, two of whom she'd grown especially close to.

After stopping by the market and running a few errands, she pulled into the parking lot. She hadn't been back to the Sheltering Arms since the day she'd been fired, and while everything inside her urged her to stay away, she couldn't just abandon Sam Darnell, the elderly man who reminded her of her great-grandfather, a one-time rodeo cowboy who'd passed away just weeks after losing his wife of fifty-eight years.

Sam had been a cowboy, too, although he'd been a rancher and had never competed in rodeos. He and his wife, Nellie, had moved into the senior apartment complex just down the block, intending to live out their remaining years together. They hadn't wanted to be a burden on their nephew, an attorney who lived and worked in Los Angeles.

But Nellie had died in her sleep last winter, and Sam had taken her loss hard. By spring he'd moved into the assisted-living facility because he'd grown weak and unsteady on his feet. And he'd continued to decline physically to the point that he had to move into the nursing home.

Chloe had been assigned to his room, and the two of them had connected in a special way. Sam had actually begun to eat again, and she'd seen an improvement in both his attitude and his physical condition.

She'd written to him regularly since her termination, but that wasn't the same as a real visit. So she'd set aside her own uneasiness and had made the effort today.

While she'd been at the market, she'd seen a display of small potted Christmas trees. So she'd picked one up for him to keep near his bed. She'd also made a stop at Caroline's Diner, where she'd purchased blueberry muffins.

Sam and his wife had been big fans of Megan Adams, who not only had a popular booth at the Brighton Valley farmer's market, but who also supplied homemade jams and baked items for Caroline.

Megan had recently married Clay Jenkins, but she was still baking up a storm and canning her award-winning jams. From what Chloe had heard, she'd even struck a big deal to sell her products regionally through a supermarket chain.

Sam had always claimed that Megan's muffins were the best he'd ever eaten, so Chloe knew the unexpected treat would please him. She'd also picked up a muffin for Ethel Furman, another of her elderly friends.

Upon entering the lobby, which boasted a fully decorated, seven-foot noble fir with a variety of brightly wrapped presents underneath, Chloe carried the small potted tree and made her way to the elevator and rode it up to the third floor.

When the doors opened, Merrilee Turner, one of several aides who took turns manning the nurses' desk, looked up from her work. When she spotted Chloe, she offered a warm smile. "Hey, girl. It's good to see you. How's it going?"

"Fine. Thanks." Chloe wondered if Merrilee would realize she'd chosen to visit on the hospital administrator's day off. Not that the man would object to her being here. It's not as if she'd been banned from the nursing home. But she'd hoped to avoid running into him.

"I thought I'd stop in to see Mr. Darnell," Chloe said. "How's he been?"

"About the same as when you were working here. He sure brightens up when one of your cards arrives in the mail."

Then it was well worth the effort of sending them to him every few days.

Chloe scanned the corridors, hoping that Sarah Poston still worked the same split shift. No need to run into her if she didn't have to. Ever since Chloe had reported Sarah's unprofessional behavior to the administrator, a charge that hadn't been followed up on and which had resulted in Chloe being discharged, there'd been bad blood between them.

Relieved not to see the dark-haired nurse, Chloe lifted the bag that held the muffins she'd brought for her elderly friends. "I brought Sam a treat as well as something to brighten up his room."

"I'm sure he'll appreciate that."

Chloe returned Merrilee's smile, then made her way to Sam's room. When she approached his door, she could hear his television cranked up a bit too loud, something Sarah had always chided him for.

"Anyone home?" Chloe asked, as she entered the room.

The silver-haired cowboy, who'd been watching a John Wayne movie, tore his gaze from the television screen. When he saw Chloe, he broke into a full-on grin. "Well, look who's here. If it ain't my favorite gal. Where have you been keeping yourself?"

Chloe hadn't shared any of her work-related issues with him before and wasn't about to do it now. So she told him about Joe's accident, the resulting amnesia and how she'd taken him in to live with her at the Rocking C.

Sam furrowed his craggy brow and wagged an arthritic finger. "You let a stranger move in with you? That's plain foolish. You don't know anything about him."

"I know he's a friend of Dave's—and that when he served in the Marine Corps he had an impressive service record."

"Humph." Sam shook his head. "He's still a man. And you're a beautiful woman. Besides, consider your reputation."

The only reputation she was really concerned about was the one here at the Sheltering Arms, which her firing had tarnished, but she merely smiled. "I'm sure Joe will be heading back to wherever he calls home as soon as his memory returns. So there's not much chance of people talking."

"I hope you're right."

"So what does Dr. Crenshaw have to say these days? Has he been in to see you?"

"The dermatologist?" Sam clucked his tongue. "Not sure if he even graduated from medical school."

"He's definitely a real doctor—but for the record, his specialty is internal medicine, not dermatology."

"What difference does it make?" Sam's eyes twinkled. "If you ask me, they all try and skin you."

Chloe laughed. That's what she loved about Sam. He might be gruff and crotchety on the outside, but he had a dry wit that contributed to his awesome sense of humor.

They continued to chat for a while. Then, after she left him the blueberry muffin, which he set aside and promised to eat later, she gave him a hug. "I'll stop by to see you again next week."

"I hope so."

"You can count on it." She gave him one last smile, then headed down the hall to Ethel Furman's room. Ethel was another special patient—and one Chloe missed. Unlike Sam, Ethel didn't have any family to look after her. And even though she'd been a schoolteacher in Brighton Valley for more than forty years, her students rarely visited.

Chloe gave a little knock on the doorjamb, then slowly entered Ethel's room, where the frail, silver-haired lady dozed in her bed.

"Good afternoon," Chloe said.

Ethel's eyes flickered open, and she turned her head toward the doorway. A slow smile stretched across her face. "What a nice surprise. How are you, dear?"

"I'm doing well. How about you?"

"I can't complain, although I need new glasses. My eyesight isn't what it used to be, and I miss being able to read."

"Did you tell anyone?" Chloe asked, as she made her way to her friend's bedside.

"Yes, but it doesn't seem to help. Apparently, they're much too busy around here to worry about an old woman."

Chloe reached for Ethel's hand, noting the frailty of her wrist—and that it was bare. "What happened to your allergy alert bracelet?"

"The clasp is broken, so I took it off."

"But you're allergic to penicillin. It's important that you wear it."

"I mentioned something to Sarah. She said she would either get it fixed or order a new one for me."

Sarah, the incompetent nurse? Good luck with that.

"How long has it been broken?" Chloe asked.

"A week or two. I'm not sure. My memory isn't what it used to be, either."

And apparently, Sarah's wasn't any better.

"I'll talk to Merrilee," Chloe said. Sometimes it seemed that the third-floor aides were more responsive and reliant than the nurse in charge.

After giving Ethel the last muffin, Chloe promised to return for another visit. Then she gave her friend a hug and left the room. But before she could reach the safety of the elevator, she spotted the one woman she'd hoped to avoid.

Apparently, Sarah wasn't working her usual split shift today. Great. Chloe hated confrontations, and this was sure to be one.

"Well, I'll be," the dark-haired nurse said. "Look what the cat dragged in."

Chloe flinched—at least, on the inside. Then she scolded herself for letting the snide comment get to her.

Sarah crossed her arms. "I didn't expect you to come around again."

"Why not?" It wasn't as though she'd done anything wrong. "I have quite a few friends here."

Sarah made a noise that sounded like a muffled snicker.

"By the way," Chloe said, "Ethel isn't wearing her allergy alert bracelet. The clasp needs to be repaired— or she'll need a new one."

"It's been ordered."

"Maybe you should provide her with some kind of temporary—"

"That won't be necessary. Her allergy is noted in her medical record."

"Maybe so, but the bracelet serves as a reminder that would eliminate the risk of someone making a mistake."

"And that's why I ordered her a new one."

Maybe so, but Ethel had been without it for quite a while already. Chloe was about to suggest that Sarah check on it, but decided she'd said enough already. At least, about Ethel. "I hear that Sam Darnell hasn't been eating well."

"We can't force him to do something against his will. Nor do we have the time to spoon-feed him. However, we offer him a healthy plate of food at each meal. If he doesn't like the taste, it's not my fault. Besides, his family should bring him other options—just like you did with that muffin today."

So Sarah had talked to Merrilee, the aide at the desk. Or maybe she'd seen the muffin in Sam's room and he'd told her who'd brought it. Either way, she'd known that Chloe was here today. Had she come looking for her?

In the scheme of things, Chloe supposed it didn't matter. "Sam and his wife never had children. And his nephew lives out of state. Since Nellie died, he has no one nearby to worry about him. Maybe, if someone sat with him during meal-time—"

"He isn't the only patient on this floor."

No, he wasn't. But something told Chloe the old man was different from the others in the nursing facility. "Another thing you might consider is sending him back to his apartment. In a more homelike setting he might get better—and stronger."

Sarah clucked her tongue. "Aren't you full of helpful ideas. You're suggesting that we take a gamble that a move might help. And I can't do that. What if he fell and broke a hip? Besides, he can't very well return to the assisted-living complex when he's resistant to any kind of assistance."

Chloe was tempted to go over Sarah's head and report her to the administrator again for her lack of compassion and her complete disregard of the feelings and wishes of the patients. But a lot of good that had done last time. So she decided not to bother. After all, she only had the training of an aide—even though she felt more qualified than the third-floor nurse in charge of the patients she'd come to know and love.

Maybe, after she graduated from nursing school, she'd have more knowledge and would feel better about challenging the woman and facing the powers that be.

Still, that didn't mean she couldn't step up to the plate and be an advocate for both Sam and Ethel.

Especially when it seemed that Chloe was the only one they had.

The sun had begun to set by the time Chloe arrived home. After parking the old ranch pickup near the barn, she made her way to the porch. As she placed her hand on the railing, it wobbled. She made a mental note to ask Joe to fix it—if he knew how.

However, she hated to overload him with chores to do. She and Tomas might need the help, but she didn't want to ask too much of the man. Even if he didn't figure out who he was and hightail it out of here in the first rental car he came across, he was still recovering from a pretty serious head injury.

She reached for the doorknob and let herself inside. The moment she stepped into the living room, the spicy aroma of meat, tomatoes and cumin filled the air.

Apparently, Joe had been busy while she'd been gone. She wondered what he'd found to cook, especially when, after looking into the pantry earlier, she'd decided that she would have to go to the market in order to come up with an appealing menu for dinner tonight.

She placed her purse on the hutch near the front door, then scanned the living room, where several red and green plastic storage containers were stacked near the hearth.

Oh, good. He'd remembered to have Tomas bring in the Christmas decorations. Chloe might not be able to go home for the holidays, but she could at least make the best of it here on the Rocking C, just as her mother always had.

No matter where in the world her parents were stationed or who was gone on deployment, Chloe's mom, an army nurse, made sure that Christmas was a special time of the year and always did things up big. And because of her efforts and the decorations they'd transported from house to house, the spirit of the season, had always been magical and had brightened their home.

In fact, because of the transient nature of her and her husband's military careers, Captain Louella Dawson took great pains to always maintain their family traditions, including a passed down recipe for hot buttered cranberry and orange scones.

Granted, her mother's skill as a combat medic was more laudable than those of being a cook, but that didn't stop her. And those scones, which had been a family recipe for longer than anyone could remember, had become as much a part of the Dawsons' winter wonderland as Santa Claus himself.

When Chloe had talked to her parents last week, they'd been thrilled that two of their three children would be with them for the holidays. As much as Chloe would have liked to have been one of those kids, she didn't have the money for airfare to Fort Drum in New York, which was where her parents were currently assigned. And even though they would have gladly shelled out the money for her travel, Chloe needed to be independent and demonstrate that she was capable of managing her own life—as well as her diminishing bank account—even if that meant being alone during the most wonderful time of the year.

Well, maybe not *alone*.

"I'm back," she called.

Joe really ought to be in bed, resting, but the smell coming from the kitchen told her he'd kept himself busy—too busy—while she'd been gone.

"I'm in here," he said.

She followed the sound of his voice, as well as the mouthwatering aroma, and found him standing at the stove, peering into a pot.

She probably ought to chastise her patient for overdoing it, especially after he'd assured her that he wouldn't, but she was too hungry and too impressed with what he'd done to make a big deal about it.

"You obviously know how to cook," she said, as she entered the kitchen with the grocery bags in hand. "Maybe you worked in the mess hall when you were in the service."

He turned and flashed a handsome grin. "Marines call it the chow hall."

He certainly seemed to remember some things— like military terms.

"Is cooking another memory?" she asked.

He shrugged, then cocked his head as if he was thinking over the possibility. "No, just common knowledge, I guess."

"Nevertheless, something sure smells delicious."

He wiped his hands on a dish towel, then took the bags from her and placed them on the counter.

"What are you doing?" she asked.

"Just messing around."

"You're supposed to be resting."

"I must've rested too much this morning. I don't think I'm used to sitting around doing nothing all day."

Chloe looked at the way his biceps filled out the borrowed Future Farmers of America T-shirt she'd found in Dave's drawer.

Ever since she'd seen his bare chest, she'd found it impossible to stop thinking about his chiseled torso or the way his muscles rippled. He certainly looked like a man who was used to action and lots of it.

In fact, she could easily envision him lifting weights, running or kickboxing if he needed an outlet for his energy. But she never would have expected to see him in the kitchen, creating something that smelled so good that her stomach was growling.

"So you decided to do some cooking?" she asked.

"Well, I started to, but then I realized I didn't have all the ingredients I needed."

"You should have called me on my cell. I could've picked them up while I was at the market."

Joe turned off the fire on the stove. "I didn't want to bother you. Plus, I didn't know if the stores in Brighton Valley would carry what I needed. Besides, when Tomas and I brought in those Christmas decorations earlier, he mentioned that his wife had bought more than they needed last weekend. She was going to make some of the dough tonight, and he promised to bring some to me tomorrow."

The small town didn't boast a mega supermarket, but they usually kept most staples in stock. "What is Tomas supposed to bring you?"

"Masa. It's a corn dough made from hominy."

"What exactly are you trying to make?"

"Tamales," Joe said simply, as if he was making something as ordinary as a peanut butter and jelly sandwich.

"You actually know how to make tamales?"

"Strangely enough, that's another thing I know how to do. Don't ask me why because I doubt that I used to make Mexican food as a sergeant in the Marines. But when I saw all those ornaments and the nativity set, all I could think of was tamales. I must associate them with Christmas. So I decided to make some. We can eat a few tomorrow, then freeze whatever is left and have them as part of the holiday meal."

"That makes sense. I associate cranberry-orange scones with Christmas because it was a holiday tradition for my family. But…" Chloe trailed off, not wanting to risk offending her guest, who was eager to have at least a small tidbit of information from his past.

"But what?" he asked.

"Well, it's just that most of the families I know who make homemade tamales for Christmas are Hispanic. But Wilcox doesn't really strike me as a typical last name."

"That's something I thought of, too. But, let's face it. My coloring would indicate that there's some ethnic blood running through my family tree. Also, when Tomas was here earlier, he said something in Spanish. I not only understood him, but I responded."

"In Spanish?"

"Yes, so either I was adopted or my mother was a lovely little señorita who married Mr. Wilcox, which is what I'm leaning toward since I obviously grew up with that heritage."

Chloe bit her cheek so that she wouldn't reflect how sad she felt about him not having any idea who his family was, especially at this time of year. She might live far away from the Dawson clan, but at least she knew where she belonged. Joe didn't even have that.

Yet instead of blustering in frustration or sinking into a depression, the guy was in here, floating around her kitchen, trying to make the best of whatever miniscule detail he *could* recall.

She liked knowing that he was a glass-half-full kind of person. Kevin Boswell, her ex-boyfriend, had always been such a pessimist, thinking the world was out to get him. And Dave, even though he wasn't ever anything more than a friend, was always so melancholy and down that Chloe's spirits sank whenever she was around either of them.

"So, how does one make tamales?" she asked.

"I had to double-check on the internet, which brought up more recipes and instructions than you can believe. And although there are lots of different methods, the one that seemed the most familiar is a two-day process anyway. So tonight I cooked the filling with some pork I found in the freezer. We can eat some of that over the rice I made."

"Boy, you have been busy," Chloe said, her admiration growing.

"I hope you don't mind me making myself at home."

"Of course not." How could she when she saw the excitement in his eyes, something she hadn't noticed before? *"Mi casa es su casa."*

He chuckled at her attempt to speak Spanish. "Tomorrow, when Tomas brings me some masa and some corn husks, I'll be able to make the dough and assemble everything together." He replaced the lid on one of the pans he had on the stove.

She liked seeing him comfortable in the kitchen, but she was even happier to know that he'd be spending one more day in the house and not out on the ranch, trying to attempt more strenuous chores. This way, he felt useful, and they were both winners.

As she began to put away the groceries she'd purchased earlier, Joe zeroed in on the sugar, vanilla, oranges and dried cranberries.

"Is that for the scones you were talking about?" he asked.

"Yes, I thought I'd make them this evening."

"I don't suppose you'd be willing to make some cookies one of these days."

"Of course. I have some great family recipes. It wouldn't be Christmas without a variety of goodies."

At that, his eyes brightened like a child standing in front of a bakery display case.

"You must like sweets," she said.

"I think you're right."

Another memory, it seemed. But not one they could build upon.

"Do you like to bake?" he asked.

"Yes, especially at this time of year. That's why I wanted to make the scones tonight. We always used to eat them when we decorated the house for Christmas."

In all honesty, Chloe would much rather spend the day baking than making a holiday meal.

"You mentioned being hungry," he said, "and dinner is ready. Do you want to eat before you make the scones?"

"It won't take me long to whip up the dough—unless you're too hungry to wait."

"I'm okay. I ate the rest of the tuna salad for a late afternoon snack. Computer sleuthing is hard work."

"How did that go, by the way?" Chloe wished she would've thought of looking him up online yesterday, but living out at the Rocking C full-time was like being in a technological time warp.

She was usually so busy with the chores and managing the ranch that she rarely had a chance to use the old computer. She'd often thought of how getting a newer modem or laptop would help streamline the day-to-day management of the ranch, like paying bills, ordering merchandise, and cutting checks to vendors and their two employees. But at the end of the month, she couldn't justify the expense. So she was left with the antiquated system Teresa Cummings had set up at least a decade ago.

"My search went about as well as I expected," Joe said. "A big fat nada on any information about me, but I did learn some interesting things about Brighton Valley."

While she mixed the ingredients for the scones and Joe wiped down the countertops, he filled her in on what he'd discovered online.

She set the oven timer just as he finished washing the mixing bowl and the pots he'd used.

"By the way, I hope you don't mind that I got into the pantry and the freezer without asking if it was okay."

She laughed. "Even if I'd had plans to use that pork you found in the freezer or the rice and beans, I'm too hungry to object."

As he placed the bowls of food on the table, she set out the plates and silverware. Then they both took their seats.

After eating the first delicious bite and savoring the taste, she said, "You must be a chef or something in your real life. This is way too good to be chow-hall fare. What'd you put in the sauce?"

"I just threw in some seasonings I found in the spice cabinet."

He'd certainly made himself at home in what she'd once considered her domain, but if he could whip up meals like this, she'd be the last one to complain. Besides, it had been ages since someone had cooked for her. And if truth be told, she liked being a guest instead of the hostess.

As they dug into their meal and silence stretched between them, she couldn't help letting her thoughts drift to Sam, Ethel and the other patients on the third floor of the Sheltering Arms. And as she did, her worry grew.

She had to do something, but what? She no longer worked there, so her hands were tied.

"What's wrong?" Joe asked.

Had her heavy thoughts been so obvious? "Why do you ask?"

"You seem sad and preoccupied."

"I visited my friends at the nursing home today and…" She paused, wondering how much to divulge. If she confided too much in him, she'd have to tell him about being fired. And then she'd have to defend her actions, or risk having him think she was a flake or a screw up or worse. And she didn't like the idea of him questioning her abilities. So she finished the sentence she'd started. "It just makes me sad. That's all."

"I'm sorry."

"Me, too." Eager to change the subject, she added, "I picked up a Christmas tree while I was in town. Maybe, after dinner, you can help me bring it inside and decorate it."

"Sure, I'd be glad to."

As she dug back into the scrumptious meal Joe had

cooked, she pondered her usual holiday traditions. Yet for some reason, she didn't seem quite as lonely as before. Nor did she think she would miss the family Christmas in New York as much as she'd once thought she would.

She might have wanted to help Joe get through the holidays this year, but now it seemed that *he* was helping *her*.

And she looked forward to creating a few new Christmas memories—with him.

Chapter Six

The night sky provided a clear view of the stars as Joe went out to get the tree from the back of the ranch pickup.

He took a moment to study the constellations, noting both the Big and Little Dippers. Apparently he had at least some astronomical knowledge, which was another tidbit of information that hadn't been completely lost to him.

For some reason, he felt oddly at home on the Rocking C. He knew where to find things, like the mop he'd used earlier today and the ladder he'd needed so he and Tomas could climb into the hayloft for the Christmas decorations. He'd even walked right up to the container of oats and molasses, popped open the lid and scooped out a handful to feed as a treat to Lola, the mare.

In spite of the fact that Hernandez, the Rocking C foreman, hadn't given him any reason to believe he'd ever stepped foot on the ranch before, Joe still couldn't seem to kick that uncanny feeling that he had.

But if so, he didn't have a clue what the circumstances had been.

Had he worked here? Maybe even lived here? If not, he must have visited Dave and his family at least once.

As he walked out to the pickup Chloe had driven to

town earlier, a crisp winter breeze stirred up the ranch scents that seemed more and more familiar.

In spite of what Hernandez had said, somewhere along the line, Joe *had* been here.

His boots crunched along the graveled drive as he headed toward the faded green GMC Chloe had parked near the barn. Hell, even that weathered old truck looked familiar. Had he driven it before? Or had he just ridden in it?

"The tree is in the back of the pickup," Chloe had told him before heading to the kitchen to check on the scones baking in the oven.

Sure enough, there it was.

He reached in, grabbed the tree by the trunk and pulled it out. As he shook out the branches, he caught the scent of pine, which didn't provoke any memories.

He had to have celebrated Christmas before. He had a tamale recipe to prove it. He cursed the amnesia that plagued him while he carried the six-foot tree into the house. Then he placed it in the stand that had been stored in the loft with all the other holiday decorations.

Joe had no more than stepped back to check out his work when Chloe carried in a tray with two steaming cups of hot cocoa and a plate of scones.

"It's a bit crooked," she said.

"I can fix that." Joe made a few minor adjustments in the stand, then tilted the trunk slightly to the left.

"That's better," Chloe said as she set the tray on the coffee table. "I'll get some water to fill the reservoir. Then we can get started."

After she returned with a plastic pitcher, she knelt and watered the tree. When she finished, she stood and brushed her hands against her denim-clad hips. Then she began to unpack the red and green plastic storage boxes.

First they strung the lights, tiny, multicolored bulbs that blinked on and off. The ornaments came next. While they worked, they'd stop long enough to nibble on the warm, buttered scones and to sip the hot chocolate.

Joe couldn't say whether he'd ever decorated a tree before, but doing so with Chloe sure felt like a first.

"Oh, look," she said as she unwrapped the tissue from an angel. "This is the perfect tree topper. Don't you think?"

Actually, just hearing her ooh and aah over the various ornaments while her eyes lit up like a hopeful child made the entire evening seem perfect. And he couldn't help but smile. "You bet."

"Can you reach to put it up? Or should I get a chair?"

"I've got it." He took the angel from her hands and put it in place.

With that done, they both stood back and studied their handiwork.

"It's beautiful," she said, her eyes glistening.

She was beautiful—even in jeans. And he couldn't help thinking that she belonged here—on the ranch, decorating a tree and making a memory.

When it was all over—not just Christmas, but his amnesia—he'd have to ask her out, just to see her all dressed up. Maybe he'd take her to that Italian restaurant...

Wait. He could almost see an actual place in his mind, a quaint restaurant with a European flair—a mural of Venice hand-painted on a white plaster wall, dark wood tables covered with white linen, a bud vase with a single red rose, a flickering candle... Where was it? When had he seen it?

"What do you think?" she asked.

About *her*? About taking her out for a romantic evening on the town?

"I love Christmas," she said, drawing his thoughts back to reality and the subject at hand.

But he still couldn't help allowing his own musing to drift back to the romantic fantasy. "All we're missing is a little mistletoe to hang over the doorway." She flushed, and he was tempted to draw her to him anyway, to kiss her senseless. In fact, as she lifted her eyes to his, as their gazes locked, desire flared.

He had no business following through on it, though. He didn't even know where he'd been, let alone where he was going. But if she didn't stop looking at him like that...

Oh, what the hell.

"Then again, something tells me I've never needed any prompts." He stepped forward, placed his hands on her cheeks. He waited a moment, taking the time to study her eyes, her expression, checking for any sign of protest.

Instead, her chin lifted and her lips parted.

That was all the invitation he needed.

As Joe lowered his mouth to hers, Chloe's heart soared in anticipation. She really shouldn't kiss him, although for the life of her, she could no longer come up with a good reason to object. Instead, she slipped her hands around his neck and stepped into his embrace.

His lips brushed hers tentatively at first, then a second time. The whisper of his breath, the promise of what was to come, sent her senses reeling, and she was soon caught up in a swirl of heat and desire.

Goodness. The man might not recall a lot of things, but he certainly knew how to kiss.

As their tongues met and mated, she lost herself in his musky, mountain fresh scent and in his sweet, chocolate-laced taste.

Did she dare put a stop to it? Or take him by the hand and lead him to one of the bedrooms?

In truth, with her knees about to give out on her, she doubted whether she could urge her feet to take a single step.

When they finally came up for air, she had to hold on to him so she wouldn't collapse into a heap on the floor.

"I was curious," he said, his breath warm against her face. "So thanks for indulging me."

She'd been curious, too, but she was even more so now. Not about kissing, but about what other heart-spinning, soul-stirring talents Joe might have. Needless to say, he would make an incredible lover.

"Well," she said, "now you know."

"Yes, but it opened a whole other world of questions."

She released her grip on his shoulders and took a step back. "Maybe so, but I don't think we ought to ponder the answers right now."

"You're probably right." He let his own hands slip down her back, his fingers leaving a trail of heat, until he released her altogether. "You'll have to forgive me. I should have known better."

"There's nothing to be sorry for. I could have re-sisted."

Oh, yeah? a small voice asked. *That's not true.*

Okay, so she'd been a willing participant—and an active one at that.

Joe turned away and strode to the stone fireplace, where Dave's photo sat on the mantel. The young man in uniform seemed to be watching them.

Something told Chloe that Dave hadn't intended for his buddy and the woman he'd thought of as "his girl" to...

What? Kiss? Become involved?

Fat chance of that happening. Chloe was in no position to strike up a romance with anyone. Not until she moved on and established herself as a nursing student at the junior college in nearby Wexler.

And Joe had to feel the same way, since his future was even sketchier than hers—at least, until he could remember his past.

His gaze drifted to the other photos on the mantel, as if they could somehow provide him with his missing identity. She suspected that he was having some of the same thoughts she was, the same concerns.

"Would you like some more cocoa?" she asked, pretending as if the kiss hadn't happened, as if she wasn't confused by all the feelings and desires it had sparked.

"Sure," he said. "Why not?"

Why not indeed? They obviously needed a distraction or something to help them cool off. She offered him a smile. "I'll just be a minute."

"While you're gone, I'll see if there are any good movies on television."

She supposed that watching TV was as good an idea as any. Yet as she left Joe to surf the channels, her thoughts made a complete one-eighty.

Too bad she wasn't free to pursue the attraction that

raged between them. But only a fool would pin her hopes and dreams on a man who knew nothing about his past, very little about his present and had no idea where the future would take him.

A noise—either real or imagined—jolted Chloe from a sound sleep, and she shot up in bed, her heart pounding as though it might jump out of her chest. She scanned the room, her eyes desperately trying to adjust to the darkness.

She didn't hear anything but the tick-tock of the clock on the bureau, so she assumed all was well and that she'd only been dreaming. That, she supposed, was the result of being overly tired.

She and Joe had turned in just before eleven o'clock. Yet, try as she might, she couldn't find a comfortable spot on the mattress. At least, not while their blood-stirring kiss continued to haunt her thoughts.

As it was, she hadn't drifted off to sleep until well past midnight.

"No!" Joe yelled from the guestroom down the hall, setting Chloe's fight-or-flight response on high alert.

"Fall back!" he shouted.

He must be having a nightmare. She glanced at the clock on the bureau. It was 3:17.

"Don't!" Joe called out again.

She threw off her blankets, rolled out of bed and hurried down the lighted hallway to the room where he slept. She stood before the closed door for a moment, her escalated pulse throbbing, her fist lifted and prepared to knock.

A moan sounded from within, and she rapped lightly.

Instead of answering, Joe yelled, "Down, dammit. Get down!"

Was he dreaming? Or was he reliving a memory?

She opened his door, allowing the light from the hall to spill inside, and watched as he thrashed around on the bed.

"Medic," he groaned.

She crossed the hardwood floor in her bare feet, then touched his shoulder, felt the warmth of his skin, the bulk of his muscles.

"Joe?" she said softly, not wanting to startle him.

Still, he lurched up on the mattress, the blanket dropping to his waist. His chest was broad—and bare—his breathing ragged. He glanced around the room as if desperate to make sense of it all.

"It's okay," she said. "You were having a nightmare."

Although his eyes were open and she suspected he was awake, he couldn't seem to blink away the fear, the confusion.

Her hand lingered on his shoulder, then trailed down a bulging biceps—the one with the military insignia—until it rested on his forearm.

Finally, his gaze cleared and he zeroed in on her, snagging something deep inside and giving it a squeeze.

"Where am I?" he asked.

Her heart went out to him. "You're at the Cummings ranch. And you were...dreaming." She reached for the glass of water he must have placed on the bedside table before retiring this evening and handed it to him.

She watched him take a long swig, watched the muscles along his throat contract. "Do you want to talk about it?"

"Not really." He raked his hand through his hair.

"I can understand," she said. "But maybe if you do, I can help you to make sense of it."

He set the water glass on the nightstand, his fingers trembling a bit as he did. Then he reached for her hand and gripped it tightly in his. "Don't leave yet."

She wouldn't consider abandoning him in a strange house and an unfamiliar bed, especially after everything he'd been through. So she took a seat on the mattress.

With his free hand, the one she wasn't holding, he threw the covers off his left leg, which was the one farthest from her hip. Then he reached down and massaged his knee. Was he wearing briefs or boxers under the blanket that barely covered him now? She supposed it didn't matter. Yet she couldn't help wondering if he was naked.

She glanced down at the flimsy gown she wore, wishing she'd taken the time to throw on a robe. But she'd been so startled by his outburst, so concerned about him, that she'd rushed to his side without thinking. That shouldn't be a problem, though. Joe was probably so caught up in that frightening nightmare that he hadn't noticed. Or maybe he didn't care either way.

"What were you dreaming about?" she asked.

He stretched out his left leg, extending his knee. "About the day I got this injury, I think. Although I can't be sure."

"From the words you said, I gathered that you were on a battlefield. You even called for a medic."

"Yeah. I was in battle. And Dave was with me."

"So you were in the same platoon?"

"I'm not sure about that. Maybe. But I was looking at that photo of him on the mantel earlier and trying hard to remember his face. So it's possible that his image only infiltrated my dream. And that none of it had been real." He blew out a ragged sigh. "But as much as I hate living with amnesia, I hope it wasn't a memory. I'd rather not think that I actually lived through that."

She could understand how he felt. But in a way, she hoped he had. And that the other memories would soon follow.

Joe lay back on his pillow, but he didn't release her hand. "I suspect it was real, though. We were under attack. And I'm pretty sure it was Afghanistan. This may sound weird to you, but I remember several phrases in an Afghani dialect. How else would I know that?"

She had no idea, but she said, "It makes sense that you would."

Once he started to talk, the tension in his body eased and his breathing slowed. Yet he still didn't let go of her hand.

She felt a yawn coming on and tried to stifle it to no avail.

"I'm sorry," he said.

"About waking me up? Don't be. I'm sure that dream was troubling. And if it helps having someone to talk to, I'm happy to be here."

"It does help. But you're tired. Go on back to bed."

She couldn't do that. Not when she knew he hadn't wanted to be alone. She might be tired, but she'd feel pretty selfish if she left him. "Is it okay if I just lie down next to you for a while?"

He scooted to the side, making room for her. So she stretched out on the mattress, on top of the covers so that their bodies were separated by the bedding. He seemed to take comfort in having her near and in whatever emotional solace she was providing.

If truth be told, she found lying next to him to be a bit comforting, too. She liked holding his hand and breathing in his masculine scent.

She wished she could help him sort through the puzzle pieces, but she couldn't.

As he continued to drift off, his breathing low and deep, the masculine timbre lulled her, sending her off to dreamland. Only her nocturnal visions weren't the least bit frightening.

She dreamed of a handsome soldier who'd just returned from war, of joining him in bed, cuddling next to him.

And as his arm draped her waist, as he drew her close, she breathed in the scent of bath soap and musk and slept peacefully until dawn chased away the night.

A pounding on the front door jarred Joe from his sleep, although the petite blonde in his arms had already awakened everything below his waist.

If the damn knocking would stop, he could focus on sexy Chloe and the fact that she was all soft and warm and curled up beside him in bed. But he couldn't take advantage of the sleeping woman who'd only climbed in next to him last night to comfort him after his nightmare.

Besides, whoever was at the door was obviously on a mission and wasn't leaving any time soon.

He rolled to the side, slipped out of the bed and pulled on the jeans he'd worn yesterday. Then he grabbed a clean shirt from the stack of clothes Chloe had left for him. He didn't realize it until he was about to open the door that the writing on the front of the snug T read: BVHS Marching Band—Drummers Bring the Boom.

Great. Now someone would think that he was a band geek, too.

He made his way to the living room. When he pulled open the front door, he found Sheriff Hollister standing on the stoop.

Joe greeted him, then stepped aside and allowed the lawman to enter. "You want some coffee?"

"Only if you have some already made."

Chloe was still asleep, so there was no way she'd risen early to put on a pot. But Joe didn't want to give off the appearance that he and the lady of the house had been up lolling around in bed together until—he peered at the grandfather clock in the living room— 0900 hours.

Damn. He never slept that late. But then again, once Chloe had climbed into his bed, he'd crashed.

"I'm sorry," Joe said. "I just woke up. But Chloe might have made some already. And if she didn't, I'll make a pot."

He hoped he'd convinced the sheriff that he had no idea where his benefactor was. The last thing he wanted to do was ruin her reputation. Assuming, of course, that she had one to ruin.

Wow. Where had that crazy thought come from? Why wouldn't she have a reputation to ruin?

As the two men filed into the kitchen, Joe got started on brewing a fresh pot while Hollister took a seat at the table.

"I take it you have more news," Joe said.

"I'm afraid so."

Joe expected the sheriff to expound on that, but he

held back when Chloe came into the kitchen wearing her standard jeans and a pink long-sleeved T-shirt. She looked far more rested and a lot less tousled than Joe felt.

Hopefully, Hollister wasn't so astute that he'd realize they'd woken up together.

"Good morning," Chloe said. "Did you uncover any more information, Sheriff?"

Hollister leaned back in his seat. "According to my friend at NCIS, Joe and Dave served in the same squad. They were both injured in the line of duty and sent to a hospital in Germany to recover. Since Dave was in worse shape than Joe, they were medically discharged at different times."

"So what's the bad news I'm sensing?" Joe asked.

Hollister took a deep breath, then slowly let it out. "Dave Cummings is dead."

The news hit Joe hard, but he turned to Chloe, who'd paled considerably. Her hand was on her chest, the fingers splayed over her heart. And her eyes glimmered with tears that threatened to spill out at any time. "What happened? Was it a result of his war injuries?"

"Not that I know of," Hollister said. "I'm still investigating that."

The coffee machine pinged, signaling it had finished brewing. Joe poured them each a cup. He laced one with cream and sugar, just the way Chloe drank hers yesterday morning, then handed it to her.

She thanked him before focusing her attention back on the sheriff.

What was she thinking? How was she really taking the news? Was she grieving for Dave, the man she'd claimed was a family friend?

"Joe, would you mind pouring the sheriff a cup of coffee?" Chloe asked.

Crap. He'd been so caught up in the news and in trying to jar his fragile memory that he'd forgotten to serve anyone other than Chloe.

"Don't bother," Hollister said. "Not unless you have a to-go cup. I have a lot going on today and need to head back to town."

"There are some disposable cups in the cupboard over the fridge," Chloe said.

Joe reached for one, then filled it with coffee for the lawman. "Cream or sugar?"

"Neither, thanks. Just black."

This time, as the sheriff headed for the door, Joe followed him out. "Thanks for coming by, even if the news was bad. I appreciate your efforts to help."

"You're welcome. It's part of the job. I just hope things work out for you. And sooner, rather than later."

"I'd been meaning to ask," Joe said. "Whatever happened to my rental car?"

"Last I heard, it was parked at the county impound lot. You'd paid two weeks in advance. You can pick it up whenever you want to. The rental company would probably be willing to send someone to collect it, though, if you're not up to driving yet."

Joe nodded, still trying to take it all in. What had he planned to do in town for so long? Or did he have other places to go?

"I think a trip to Houston is in order," Joe said. "I'd like to see what I can find out on my own. You think your buddy at NCIS would be willing to talk to me?"

"He said he's always willing to help out a fellow devil dog. But he said that he's only at liberty to divulge so much info." Hollister reached into his pocket, pulled out a couple of business cards. When he found the one he was looking for, he handed it to Joe. "Here's his office address. I'll call ahead and let him know you're coming by."

"Thanks." Joe studied the card for a moment, then added, "I doubt he'll be able to tell me anything more than he's already told you, but I'd still like to find out more about Dave—and what happened to him."

"So would I."

Joe stiffened. "You don't think his death had anything to do with me being hit by a car, do you?"

"I don't like to leave stones unturned. However, I doubt that the two incidents are related. In the meantime, we've contacted all the local companies who do bodywork on vehicles. If the driver who hit you was one of the locals and had been drinking at the bar, he might have left the scene so he could avoid getting slapped with a DWI. We might be able to find him that way."

"Him? It was a man?"

"The woman who placed the 9-1-1 call said she didn't see the driver or the vehicle. But there was another witness down the street who said the driver was a male in a Silverado pickup. So we're following up on that lead."

"So you'd still rather I didn't go into Brighton Valley?"

"Not yet. But I hope to have some solid answers soon."

Joe nodded, then thanked Hollister again and waited until he'd driven away.

Moments later, when Joe returned to the kitchen, he found Chloe seated at the table, deep in thought. He noted her stricken expression, the way she nibbled on her bottom lip.

What was wrong? Was she grieving for Dave?

"Are you okay?" Joe asked.

She glanced up and forced a smile. "Yes. I'm just feeling…sad. I hadn't even considered that Dave…" She blew out a sigh. "I'll be fine."

"I'm sorry," he said, wondering why he wasn't as grief stricken as she seemed to be. Probably because he still couldn't remember the guy who was supposed to be his buddy.

They said war was hell. But so was amnesia.

"Apparently," Chloe said, "that dream you had last night was real—and probably a flashback of some kind."

"I think you're right."

Her expression softened. "Maybe your memory will slowly return through your dreams."

"As much as I want to kick the brain fog, I'm not sure I want to be plagued with another nightmare."

She smiled, a rosy hue coloring her cheeks and brightening her eyes.

Was she thinking about how his arms had felt around her while they'd slept? If so, then another nightmare might be his undoing.

Especially if she spent another night in his bed.

Chapter Seven

Chloe studied the coffee mug in her hand, trying to gather her thoughts after the unexpected turn of events.

Just fifteen minutes earlier, when the morning sun filtering through the blinds had lit the guest room, she'd stretched and yawned. Then she'd rolled to the side and glanced across the mattress, only to find the spot where Joe slept empty, the sheets and blanket tousled.

She'd caught the scent of coffee in the air and assumed he was in the kitchen, fixing breakfast. So she'd climbed out of bed and padded down the hall to her own bedroom. Since she'd showered last night, before turning in, she'd dressed quickly and run a brush through her hair.

Sometime during the wee hours of the morning, Joe had slipped his arms around her and drawn her close. Well, as close as the blanket between them would allow. That intimacy—as well as the memory of the heated kiss they'd shared earlier—urged her to find him, to talk to him.

Would he feel better about sharing the details of that nightmare with her in the light of day? Had the dream triggered any of his memories?

She'd entered the kitchen with a spring in her step and a smile on her lips. And when she'd spotted Sheriff Hollister seated at the table, talking quietly to Joe, her mood had soared. Her hopes, too, as she'd waited to hear the news he'd brought.

But as he told them why he'd come, what he'd learned, a dark cloud of emotion hovered over her. Grief, doubt, worry and even a splash of guilt, all weighed her down.

Dave was *dead*.

She could hardly believe it. She grieved for him, of course—for the loss of his life. But learning that he was never coming home troubled her for more reasons than one.

What was she going to do about the ranch? The bills had been mounting, and last year's taxes had yet to be paid. She'd written to Dave, sharing her fears and hoping he'd offer some direction, telling her just what he wanted her to do in his absence.

But instead of an answer, her unopened letter had made its way back to the ranch. And now she knew why. The military must have assumed that Dave had gone home after his discharge. But somewhere along the way he'd died.

A nagging suspicion, a suffocating sense of remorse, threatened to drag her down even more. What if Dave had committed suicide? And what if Chloe's rejection had contributed to the despondence that had led him to end it all?

His letter to her, the one Joe had delivered, had been cryptic, his parting words so…final.

But if you're not interested in what we could have together, then I won't bother you again. Goodbye. Dave.

Had he hoped that she'd go looking for him? That

she'd tell him she'd changed her mind rather than risk losing him?

Chloe wouldn't have done that. She hadn't wanted to hurt Dave, but she would never marry a man she didn't love. Yet that didn't stop the grief—or the worry.

Maybe she should search the house to find a solution to the problems at hand. Had Teresa hidden money to use for a rainy day? If so, this would certainly be that day.

Teresa had also had a will. She'd told Chloe about it and had mentioned that her attorney, who had an office in Wexler, kept a copy of it in his files.

After her friend's funeral, Chloe had contacted the man, and he'd guided her and Dave through the process of transferring ownership of the ranch to Dave. He'd also drawn up the paperwork that had given Chloe power of attorney so she could keep the ranch going until Dave returned from deployment.

Did Dave have a will, too? If so, that would give Chloe some idea who should be notified, who would be able to look after the ranch now.

But unless she could find someone to hand the reins to, she couldn't very well leave. What would happen to Tomas and the other ranch hands? And what about the cattle and horses?

No, she needed to stay until the legalities were sorted out and settled. And while she really didn't have a place to go, she did have plans and dreams.

And sadly, as long as she stayed on the Rocking C she'd never be able to pursue her degree in nursing or to get on with her life. She may have wanted to settle down in one place, but she didn't want to be *stuck* there. And that's how she was beginning to feel.

"Will you excuse me?" she asked Joe without waiting for a reply.

Then she took her coffee mug and headed to the den to see what she could find.

Joe watched Chloe leave the kitchen in somber silence. She probably needed to grieve and wanted to do so alone. He couldn't blame her for that.

So he poured himself another cup of coffee and set about fixing breakfast—scrambled eggs and ham.

When it was ready and the table had been set, he went in search of her. He'd expected to find her holed up in her room, crying. But when he heard the sound of rustling papers in the den, he proceeded toward the open door.

He found her seated at the desk, where paperwork littered the polished oak surface. She had her back to him and was leaning to the side, digging through a drawer of files.

She didn't appear to be grieving, as he'd expected. Instead, she seemed to be looking for something.

"What's up?" he asked.

She stiffened, as though he'd caught her in the act of...well, hell, he didn't know what.

"Oh!" She lifted her head and glanced over her shoulder, her eyes wide, lips parted and cheeks flushed a pretty shade of pink. "I didn't hear you come in."

She'd been too intent in her search, he supposed.

"I fixed breakfast," he said. "It's ready whenever you are."

She glanced at the paperwork on the desk, then turned her gaze back on him. "I'll be there in a minute."

"Looking for something?"

She bit down on her bottom lip. Was she wondering if she could trust him with the answer? Or was she feeling guilty for sifting through the ranch files?

"Just some paperwork," she said.

"Need some help?"

"No, I've got it."

He nodded as though it made perfect sense. And in a way, he supposed it did. She'd been holding down the home front while Dave was away. And so she worked in here. Still, she'd looked a little sheepish when he'd found her.

Unable to quell his curiosity, he asked, "Does this have anything to do with the letter he wrote?"

"No. It's just ranch business."

He waited a moment, hoping she'd say something about the letter, about the contents. He wanted to know what was so important that he'd made a possible death-bed promise to deliver it.

When she didn't respond, his curiosity morphed into suspicion, although he couldn't exactly say why.

He nodded toward the doorway. "Well, since you're busy, I'll head back into the kitchen and leave you to your work."

"Thanks. I'm about done here."

As Joe turned to go, he couldn't quite shake his uneasiness. But then again, what did it matter? His amnesia had left him unsettled about a lot of things.

Joe had barely returned to the kitchen when Tomas arrived, bringing corn husks and the masa his wife had made. Joe thanked the foreman and paid him the cost of the needed items. Then he placed the dough in the refrigerator so he could make the tamales later in the day. Next, he fixed breakfast for two.

He'd just scooped out a heaping spoonful of scrambled eggs onto his plate when Chloe returned to the kitchen.

"That sure smells good," she said. "I still think you may have gone to culinary school."

Unfortunately, Joe had no clue about whether he had or hadn't. He took a slice of ham from the skillet, then carried his meal to the table. Chloe joined him and they ate in relative silence.

As she picked up their empty plates, Joe asked, "Do you mind if I borrow the ranch truck for the day?"

Her motions slowed to a stall. "The sheriff suggested that you stay on the ranch. And as far as I know, he didn't say anything about that changing. Where did you want to go?"

"To Houston. I'd like to do a little recon work on my identity."

"Did he provide you with any more to go on while the two of you were outside?"

"No. But I want to follow through on the military lead."

"That makes sense. And with Houston being nearly two hours from here, it's not likely anyone from Brighton Valley will see you. So sure. Go ahead."

"Thanks."

He turned to leave the room, but she reached for his arm and stopped him. "Would you like me to ride with you?"

He probably ought to tell her he'd rather be alone. But that wasn't true. For some reason, it seemed as though he'd spent the bulk of his life alone. And he wanted that—no, he needed that—to change.

So he offered her a smile. "Sure, why not?"

When she returned his smile and gave his arm a gentle squeeze, he realized that he was actually glad to have her come along.

Twenty minutes later, she'd changed into a pair of black slacks that rode low on her hips, a white blouse and a pale green sweater. She'd woven her long hair into a twist that was held by a silver clip and had applied lipstick.

Looked like the cowgirl had morphed into a stylish lady who'd blend in nicely with the city folk.

No, someone as pretty as Chloe would stand out in a crowd, no matter what she did to her appearance.

"Thanks for waiting," she said. "You ready to go?"

"Yep."

As she headed for the back door, he followed her and watched as she snagged the key ring off the hook on the mudroom wall. Once they were both outside, she led the way to the ranch pickup and opened the driver's door.

He could have asked her to let him drive, but he sat back and let her take the wheel. Being the passenger would give him a chance to check out the scenery and to see if something along the way would jog his memory.

He didn't like the idea of taking the old ranch truck such a long distance in case it broke down. He considered suggesting that they stop by the county impound lot to pick up his rental car, but on the outside chance that someone was actually looking for him, they'd be watching for a nondescript four-door sedan.

So it was Ol' Greenie that chugged along the county road, which would lead them to the interstate.

Wait. How had he known the pickup's nickname?

The answer came to him as quickly and as naturally as Ol' Greenie had. He'd remembered a distinct voice—*Dave's* voice?—referring to the beat-up ranch truck that way.

Joe stole a glance across the seat at Chloe, wondering if she could verify what had surely been a memory.

"Does this truck have a nickname?" he asked.

She shot a glance across the seat. "Why do you ask?"

"I think it does, and I want to check my memory."

"Dave used to call it Ol' Greenie."

Joe nodded. "That's what I thought."

As they continued on their way, they approached a park near Wexler. The playground was empty, yet Joe imagined—remembered?—a handful of barefoot kids wearing shorts and playing in those same fountains. He also envisioned a piñata hanging from the gazebo rafters. A birthday celebration, it seemed. But whose?

For some reason, he thought it might have been his.

He nearly mentioned that to Chloe, but why? One—or possibly two—little memory fragments certainly didn't mean much. He'd better wait until he had more to go on. But if he actually had played in that park as a kid, then he'd probably lived close by.

Had he and Dave been childhood friends? It would stand to reason. And if that was the case, then that would explain why Tomas, who'd come to work at the Rocking C four or five years ago, hadn't remembered ever seeing him. Maybe Joe and his family had moved away by that time.

Damn. He hated having to piece together bits and pieces of memory when he had no way of knowing how much—or if any of it—was right or wrong.

Chloe merged onto the interstate that would take them to Houston. They'd both kept pretty quiet since they'd driven off, instead letting Garth Brooks and Alan Jackson do the talking—or rather, the singing—for them.

When they finally pulled off the freeway, Joe checked the address on the business card Sheriff Hollister had given him.

"I know where that street is," Chloe said. Then she headed toward the NCIS office.

They parked and went inside the building. When they stopped by the reception desk, they asked for Agent Mike Danielson, the man who held more answers about Joe's identity than Joe did himself.

Moments later, Danielson greeted them in the lobby. The gray-haired agent had to be pushing sixty years old, but his appearance gave credence to that old adage, "Not as lean, not as mean, but still a marine."

"Nice to meet you," Danielson said before shaking hands with them both. "Shane called me and told me you were heading over here, so I got together as much information for you as I could. I even made some copies of the non-classified stuff in case you need that later on."

He escorted them to a cubicle office and pulled an extra chair over for Chloe. Then he handed a file to Joe. "Here's your discharge paperwork and some write-ups you had for your more recent medals."

Joe scanned the list of commendations he'd received during his years in the service, but he was more interested in his personal information than he was in his service record.

He'd joined the military six months after his eighteenth birthday, which was July 7, the same date that was listed on his California driver's license.

Danielson confirmed that Joe had never reported being married or otherwise having any dependents. "Of course, you could have gone AWOL and gotten married," the older man said. "But it seems like a soldier with your proven track record would have followed the rules and reported any changes to the appropriate channels. Besides, your emergency contact is listed as Stanley J. Conway in El Paso. His information is there if you want to take it, but I already tried to call him for you and his voice mailbox was full so we couldn't leave a message."

Joe wondered how he knew the man with a different last name. Didn't he have *any* relatives? He asked Danielson that same question.

"I did a little snooping and ran Conway's name through our database. I can't give you any information about a fellow marine, even though he's retired and has no listed relatives, either."

Joe understood immediately that the agent was letting him know that his next of kin was actually an older marine with no family to speak of. Clearly, Joe wasn't related to the man by blood, but apparently this guy was the closest thing he had to a family.

So where had the tamale recipe come from, not to mention that birthday party and the piñata memory, if Joe didn't have any relatives of his own? Had his family members died?

"What about David Cummings?" Chloe asked.

Joe wasn't surprised by her interest in finding out more information about her "family friend." He'd been watching her closely since she'd gotten the news of Dave's death. Granted, he didn't really know Chloe very well, but he could definitely spot a look of uneasiness on someone's face.

He'd seen her expression when she was sad, and he'd seen her confused. But up until this morning, he'd yet to see her look guilty.

Was that because she and Dave had been more than friends? And that before she'd known of his death, she'd kissed Joe?

Or did that have to do with whatever paperwork she'd been looking for today?

"I'm not at liberty to give you guys access to Corporal Cumming's file," Danielson said. "But off the record, he was injured by the same snipers who shot your knee."

Danielson told them that Joe and the men in his squad had been bunkered behind an overturned minibus in the middle of Helmand Province. They'd been under fire from Taliban insurgents carrying assault rifles and hiding in an abandoned apartment building. The communications specialist had radioed for backup.

"Before anyone arrived," Danielson said, "one of your men charged the snipers. He took down one of them, but was severely wounded. You followed him, grabbed him by the back of his pack and pulled him to safety—in spite of the fact that you took a bullet in the knee."

So that's how Joe had been wounded.

"Who was the man I went after?" Joe asked.

"David Cummings. His injuries were even more serious than yours, and by the looks of the report, you saved his life."

Too bad he didn't remain alive long enough to enjoy it.

"After you recovered in Germany," Danielson added, "you were medically discharged and returned to the States. Cummings was discharged later since his injuries were much more serious."

"So then he didn't die from his battle wounds?" Chloe asked.

"Negative. The coroner in San Diego notified us of his death and sent us the death certificate so that we could terminate disability benefits. My suggestion would be to contact them to get an autopsy report or death certificate for yourselves."

Joe could barely process what the agent had told them about Dave because he was still reading the incident report of what had happened in Afghanistan. Fragments of his dream began to make sense.

"That's all I've got for you," Danielson said as he politely extracted the confidential report from Joe's hand. "Good luck with that whole amnesia thing. If I hear anything else, I'll keep you posted."

Chloe thanked Danielson for his time and nudged Joe with her elbow. Apparently he'd been so wrapped up in his own thoughts that he hadn't noticed the NCIS agent trying to graciously end the meeting.

Danielson held out his hand, and Joe shook it.

"No matter what else you find out about your identity," Danielson said, "you're a hero, son."

Funny, but for some reason, Joe didn't feel like one.

As he and Chloe left the office and climbed back into Ol' Greenie, they both remained silent. He figured there was almost too much to say, but neither of them wanted to share their thoughts out loud.

Chloe started the engine and backed out of the parking space. Before she headed onto the street, she glanced across the seat at Joe. "Do you mind if we do a little shopping while we're here?"

"No, not at all." In fact, after talking to Danielson, he'd welcome a distraction. "What do you need to buy?"

"I already shipped gifts home to my parents, but I'd like to pick up a few last-minute presents for some of my friends."

He should have realized that she had a social life. A beautiful woman like her would.

"So what are we looking for? Clothes, perfume...?" He tossed her a grin as he dug for a little more information. "Aftershave?"

"Actually, I'm not sure what to get for them. They're both in a nursing home. Do you have any ideas?"

"Nope. Not a single one." Something told him he didn't usually get caught up in the Christmas spirit. "But I'm more than willing to help you shop. That is, as long as you don't make me carry your purse."

She laughed as she pulled out of the parking lot and headed toward the heart of downtown.

Now that he thought about it, Joe was glad they were going shopping. If he was going to spend Christmas with Chloe, he'd like to get her a gift.

As they chugged and rumbled along, he glanced at the discharge paperwork he still held and at the contact info for Stanley Conway. He'd have to call the guy who might be able to fill in even more details of his life.

Did he actually want to stick around in Brighton Valley? He knew enough about himself and had the means to leave and find his way home to California.

But when he stole a glance at the beautiful blonde humming along to a George Strait song on the old truck's FM dial, when he remembered the kiss they'd shared last night—and waking with her in his arms this morning—he realized that he wasn't quite ready to leave just yet.

By the time Chloe and Joe found the shopping district, it was early afternoon. She hadn't eaten much at breakfast and hunger pangs reminded her of that fact. Maybe she should suggest they eat while they were in town.

She snagged a parking space close to The Cowboy Connection, the store she'd wanted to visit, and shut off the ignition. As they climbed from the truck, she caught the aroma of grilled meat and barbecue sauce.

"Do you smell that?" Joe asked.

"I sure do." Chloe scanned the area and spotted Earl's Smokehouse, a restaurant across the street with a green door and a black, wrought iron railing around the outdoor curbside tables.

"Are you hungry?" he asked.

"Sounds like you are," she said with a smile. "And if you're talking about eating at Earl's, I'm game."

"You read my mind. The tables outside are empty, probably because of the chill. But look in the window. The place is packed. I'll bet it's really good."

"You're probably right. But then again, this is Texas. And we know good barbecue when we taste it."

"Then what are we waiting for?"

They crossed the street, and when they reached the green door, Joe opened it and stepped aside so Chloe could enter first.

They were greeted by a smiling, middle-aged brunette wearing a red-and white-checkered shirt and jeans. "Hey, y'all. Two for lunch?"

When Joe told her yes, she snagged the menus. "Come with me."

Once they were seated at a small booth in back, Joe said, "I think I grew up in Texas."

"Why is that?"

"Because I really have a hankering for barbecue beef, as if it's always been my favorite meal. Well, that and Mexican food."

"That's certainly possible," Chloe said. "But there has to be more reason for you to think that other than your food choices."

"There are, but it's more of a feeling right now. I can't explain it."

When the same waitress who'd seated them came by to take their orders, Chloe chose the chicken salad and a glass of sweet tea.

"I'll have tea, too," Joe said. "And for lunch, I'd like the sampler platter with potato salad, French fries and coleslaw. Plus a side of cornbread."

Chloe's jaw dropped. "Are you sure you want that sampler? I think it's meant for two or more people to share. It comes with three different kinds of meat."

Joe chuckled. "I guess I have a big appetite."

And he'd been right because, when the waitress brought the food on the large metal plates, he ate every last bite.

"How was it?" Chloe asked.

"Great. I'd come back."

When the bill came, Chloe reached for it, but Joe grabbed her wrist. "Oh, no, you don't." He continued to hold her arm while he used his free hand to pull out his wallet. "You drove, so I'm paying for lunch."

"Are you sure? You might need that money for something else."

"Like what?"

She laughed. "Like the ingredients to make a whole lot more tamales. With the way you can put away food, you must spend a fortune on groceries."

"Funny thing is, I still have room for dessert."

"I wouldn't be surprised to find out that you're a born Texan. Only someone from the Lone Star state can love brisket that much."

He smiled at her attempt at levity, then sobered. He supposed it was time to talk about the big white elephant sitting at the table with them. So he stroked her fingers softly, broaching that physical connection they'd had earlier and the attraction that had been brewing ever since they'd kissed last night. "How are you feeling about everything?"

"I'm sad about Dave," she said. "I'd expected him to come back to the ranch soon, and I'm in limbo."

"Why is that?"

Chloe pondered the question as well as her answer, since she didn't want to dump any more on Joe than she had to. "Because I don't want to move until the new owner is located."

"New owner?"

"Whoever stands to inherit the ranch now that Dave is gone." She figured that was enough of an explanation. "How about you? Are you feeling badly about Dave's death?"

"I don't know. I don't feel any differently than I did yesterday. If we were friends, and I'm beginning to believe that we were, I should be sad about his death.

But maybe because I don't remember him it hasn't really hit me yet."

"That's probably true."

"There might be another reason for it," he added. "If he gave me that letter before he died and I carried out his wish, it's possible I already knew about his death before coming here. And if that's the case, then maybe I've already done my grieving."

"Did Sheriff Hollister mention when Dave died?" Chloe asked, realizing she should have quizzed the sheriff.

"No. But that ought to be easy enough to figure out. We can check with the coroner in San Diego—or ask Hollister what they told him."

When the waitress returned with their change, Joe left a generous tip.

"Dr. Nielson was probably right," he said as he got to his feet. "I need to be patient and wait for my brain to heal and my memory to return. So let's enjoy our time in Houston and make the most of the rest of the day."

Chloe forced a smile, then stood. After they left the restaurant, they walked to The Cowboy Connection, a department store that catered to those who liked Western wardrobes and home decor.

The store had been adorned with wreaths and expensive ornaments, and Christmas music filled the air. Her mood continued to lift—no doubt due to the holiday spirit.

While they walked past displays that provided more than a few gift ideas, Joe helped her choose a bronze horse figurine for Sam Darnell.

Next she found a pair of pajamas for Ethel Furman. As she waited to pay the clerk for her purchase in the lingerie department, she glanced over to a display where Joe stood, fingering the silky fabric of a skimpy black nightie and studying it intently.

Had another memory returned? If so, Chloe couldn't find it in herself to be happy for him. She'd wanted him to remember the life he'd led before coming to Brighton Valley. But she certainly hadn't wanted him to remember a particular woman dressed in something so sexy.

When he turned toward the cash register where she stood, waiting in line to make her purchase, their gazes met and locked.

And for one magical moment, she wished she'd been the woman he was trying so hard to remember.

Chapter Eight

Joe hadn't expected Chloe to catch him looking at the sexy lingerie on display, let alone fondling them. So the moment their eyes met, he felt like a kid who'd been caught with his hand in the candy bowl.

Had she known that he'd been thinking of buying one of those skimpy nighties for her? That he'd envisioned her sitting on the side of his bed, like she had last night, only dressed in a whisper of black silk instead of a cotton gown? Not that the thin cotton hadn't been just as sweet and sensual to look at—just in a different sort of way.

He'd better put some distance between her and his lust-filled thoughts before he asked her to try on something for size. So he let the slinky fabric slip out of his hand and said, "If you don't mind, I'm going downstairs to check out the menswear. I need to buy some clothes that fit me better than jeans with a thirty-inch inseam and old high school T-shirts that make me look like a band geek." Then he headed for the escalator before she could answer.

She must have gotten sidetracked with another purchase, because by the time she found him in the shoe department, where he was trying on a pair of cowboy boots, he'd already bought three pairs of jeans and several work shirts. She took the seat next to him and glanced at the shopping bags on the floor. "I see you've been busy."

"It's easy when there's a good selection."

"That's why I love this store. Every time I come in here, I want a ranch of my own. I didn't grow up around horses, but I must be a cowgirl at heart."

"I thought you were a nurse at heart."

"Maybe I'm both."

He stopped wrestling with the second boot long enough to cast a glance her way and catch a glimmer in her eye. "If you had a ranch of your own, would you give up nursing?"

"I don't know. Maybe. I'd probably invite some friends to live with me, so I'm not sure how much time I'd have to study."

"Which friends?"

She bit down on that bottom lip again. Then she shrugged a single shoulder. "I'm not sure. I really haven't thought much about it."

He didn't believe her. She seemed too pensive. She must have given it more than a little consideration. But he let the remark pass and removed the first pair of boots from his feet and reached for the black Ropers.

As he tried those on, Chloe stood and wandered through the women's shoe section until she stopped at a table that displayed a pair of custom stitched red boots.

"Aren't these cool? I wonder if they have them in a size six." She turned them over and glanced at the sticker price on the sole. Then she put them right back where she'd found them.

She continued to study them a moment longer, though.

He figured she couldn't afford a new pair of anything, let alone expensive leather boots. Yet here she was, shopping for gifts for her elderly friends in the nursing home. She'd also been sharing her groceries with him and shelling out gas money to drive him into Houston.

When Chloe wandered off to check out a display of slippers, Joe asked the clerk if she had those red boots in a size six. When the woman said they did, he asked her to add them to his latest purchase—the black Roper boots.

Once he'd paid for both pairs, he hid hers at the bottom of the bag that held his clothing and headed for the slipper display to join her.

"Did you find something else to buy?" he asked.

"I was looking for something to go with the nightgown I bought for Ethel. But I don't think she'll like any of these." She shifted the shopping bag she held to her other hand. "Is there something else you need?"

"A hat," he said, "especially if I'll be working on the ranch with Tomas."

"I saw them near the escalators." She bumped his arm with hers. "Come on."

He followed her to the display and considered his options. Knowing he'd soon get it dirty, he reached for a straw hat and tried it on.

He'd no more than given it a proper tilt when Chloe snatched it from his head, replaced it with a black felt Stetson and smiled. "I've always been a sucker for a man in a black hat."

"Sold." He flashed her a boyish grin, then headed for the nearest register. After paying the clerk, he decided to wear it out of the store.

As Joe and Chloe strode toward the pickup, he inadvertently bumped her shoulder. Apparently she thought he'd done it on purpose, because she smiled and bumped him right back.

"I'm glad we came here today," she said. "It's been a nice break from everything, and I had fun."

"Me, too." He felt compelled to take her hand in his, but after considering the consequences of a move like that, the possible complications, he held back.

Besides, something still wasn't quite right, leaving him completely off stride. In spite of what he'd learned at the NCIS office, he felt undeserving, not only of medals, but of the beautiful blonde who walked beside him.

Why was that?

What memories was his mind still holding hostage?

Joe had been pretty quiet on the drive home, and his pensive mood hadn't lifted, even after dinner. He'd volunteered to do the dishes, then had insisted on making the tamales on his own, saying he wanted the quiet time, hoping it would trigger some memories.

If it had, Chloe had no way of knowing, because two hours later he excused himself and turned in for the night, leaving her to watch TV alone.

It had been a long day, and she was exhausted, so she turned off the television at ten. After setting the alarm for six so she'd be the first one up, she went to bed.

She slept fairly well and, just as she'd hoped, she beat Joe to the kitchen, where she put on the coffee, then fried some turkey sausage and whipped up the pancake batter. She'd just set the table, when Joe finally entered the room.

He was sporting his new clothes and holding his hat,

which he set on the table. As he sauntered to the coffee-maker and poured himself a cup of the fresh brew, he moved with a sexy swagger that scrambled her senses.

Dang. Joe Wilcox looked better than a cowboy had a right to.

If he knew she'd been ogling him, he didn't let on. Instead, when he looked at her, he blessed her with a heart-stopping grin.

"So what's on the agenda today?" he asked.

"What do you mean?" Did he think she had another shopping trip in store for him?

"Do you have a list of things you'd like me to do? Or should I go outside and look for Tomas?"

Oh, he meant work. Actually, having him busy and out of the house would allow her more time to search the files in the den and to decide what she was going to do now that Dave wasn't coming home.

She also wanted to contact the coroner's office in San Diego and find out how she could get a copy of Dave's death certificate. She didn't know a thing about estate planning or probate court, but she was pretty sure she'd need to file some official documents with somebody. But she kept those thoughts to herself.

It wasn't that she didn't want Joe to know what she was doing. She had nothing to hide. But after the troubling dream he'd had two nights ago and their visit to the NCIS office yesterday, she figured the poor man had been through enough and she didn't want to burden him with her financial woes.

"Tomas is probably already out and about," Chloe said. "As soon as I see him, I'll ask if he has any work that needs to be done. Do you know anything about cattle or horses?"

"I'm not sure. I guess we'll find out soon enough."
He went back to eating, digging into that stack of hotcakes and syrup with the same gusto he'd shown yesterday at lunch and again last night at dinner.

Joe either had a hearty appetite or was just as anx-
ious to get to work as she was. An active man like him
had to be going stir-crazy by being cooped up indoors
with no physical outlet.

Of course, if they spent any more time alone together, Chloe might lose her head and offer to provide
him with a physical outlet of the bedroom variety.

Her cheeks warmed at the thought, and she turned
away to avoid his gaze.

When a horse whinnied outside, she looked out the
big bay window and spotted Tomas walking Lola to
the paddock. The prize broodmare had been stabled
in the barn and was expected to foal soon. He must be
exercising her.

"There's Tomas now," she said. "Why don't we go
out and ask him what needs to be done. I'll come back
and wash the breakfast dishes later."

Joe's chair scraped the tile floor as he scooted
away from the table. Then, after getting to his feet,
he snatched his hat and followed her from the kitchen,
through the mudroom and out the back door.

Once outside, he slipped on the new Stetson and
gave it a little adjustment—just like a real live Texan.

Even though his stonewashed jeans and flannel work
shirt were brand-new, they appeared to have been worn
several times before. With the added boots and hat, he
looked like the real McCoy—born and raised on the
Rocking C—and not just a city slicker who wanted to
play rancher.

Chloe hadn't meant to admire the sexy marine's transformation, but she'd always been a sucker for a handsome cowboy. And she was eager to see how he did on a horse.

She had a sneaking suspicion that he was no stranger to the ranch life. And with the way his backside filled out that denim, he was certainly no stranger to looking the part.

"Buenos dias," Joe said to Tomas.

The ranch foreman responded in Spanish. They spoke that way for a while, then lapsed into English.

If Chloe had been able to focus on more than two words at a time, she would have appreciated the switch to a language she could understand.

While they talked, she tried to get her lusty thoughts in check. Finally, she managed to tune in to the end of their conversation.

"That would be helpful," Tomas said, "if you're sure you're up for it."

Joe insisted that he was.

"Good." The foreman brightened. "Then I can stay here and work in the stables, just in case Lola needs me."

Tomas started toward the barn with Joe on his heels, and Chloe hurried to catch up—both physically and mentally. Apparently, the foreman had told Joe there'd been some damage to the fence after the last storm.

"I'll ride along the boundary of the ranch," Joe said. "If I see any damage, I'll fix it."

"If there's anything you and those tools you're carrying can't handle, just flag the spot. When you get done, I'll go back out with you."

The men made it sound like a simple task. And it

probably would be. Joe seemed hearty enough to stay in the saddle and not get lost.

"Make sure you take plenty of water with you," Chloe said, her nursing instincts finally kicking in. "Even though it's cold out, you can still get dehydrated."

Both men looked at her as though they didn't much welcome her ministrations, so she excused herself and told them she was going back inside to do the dishes.

Once that was out of the way, she went to the den. But instead of immediately dealing with the stack of bills on the desk, she stood at the window and watched Joe lead Dave's gelding out of the stable.

Fortunately, Firestorm had been named for his reddish color and not for his temperament. He was a strong and dependable horse, well-suited for ranch work. But was Joe?

Chloe knew she shouldn't worry, but as he mounted, as he threw his right leg over the saddle, she held her breath.

He settled into the saddle like a natural, then cantered around the yard, no doubt allowing the horse to get used to him—and vice versa.

When she realized that he was perfectly capable of handling the reins, she let out the breath she'd been holding. Her stance relaxed even more when Tomas handed Joe one of the ranch's walkie-talkies. At least, if he had a problem along the way, he could call for help.

Still, she stood at the window and watched until Joe and Firestorm were well out of sight. At that point, she turned back to the desk and finished the work that had piled up since Joe had arrived.

Next, she did an internet search to find contact information for the San Diego coroner's office. It was two hours earlier on the west coast, so she couldn't call yet. But fortunately she learned how to request the records she needed.

With that knowledge tucked under her belt, she searched Texas probate law. It didn't take long to realize she wasn't going to handle any of that on her own. She was in way over her head.

She checked the time—a couple of minutes after nine—and then placed a call to Jeffrey McDougall, the attorney who'd handled Teresa's estate.

Mr. McDougall was out of the office, but his secretary assured Chloe that he was familiar with the Rocking C and the Cummings family. The woman expressed her condolences over Dave's death and told Chloe that the attorney would call back the next afternoon.

After hanging up, she tackled the overdue invoices from some of the ranch's suppliers. Before mailing any payments, she would need to reconcile the Rocking C bank account and figure out how the ranch was going to pay its two employees after January rolled around.

A local rancher had offered to purchase a hundred head of cattle, but Chloe had been reluctant to accept it. She had a feeling the buyer was lowballing her—not only because she was a female, but because he knew she wasn't all that familiar with the going rate for cattle.

Unfortunately, Tomas, who'd been a ranch hand prior to stepping up to help run things when the previous foreman retired, wasn't up on fair prices, either.

But Chloe knew someone who was. The next time she stopped by the Sheltering Arms for a visit—which would be soon—she would talk to Sam Darnell about it. The old cattleman may not keep up on his food intake, but he definitely kept up on his agricultural knowledge.

By noon, Joe had crept back into her thoughts. He'd been gone for quite a while. Maybe he'd overdone it by repairing one of the fence posts that often came loose following an East Texas rainstorm.

Of course, she didn't want him to think that she doubted his ability, but she'd feel a lot better if she could check things out herself.

So she decided to fix some sandwiches and ride out to wherever he was working, under the pretext of bringing him lunch. The man never turned down food. And while he ate, his stomach would be too busy to allow his brain to question her intentions.

Ten minutes later, she delivered one of the thick ham sandwiches to Tomas, who was cleaning out the stalls in the barn. Then she saddled Rosabelle, the gentle mare she usually rode, and tied a rolled up quilt behind the saddle. When it was secure, she stowed the impromptu picnic lunch in the saddlebags.

Satisfied that she had everything she needed, she mounted Rosabelle and rode off to find Joe.

Joe had just finished restringing the lower line of barbed wire when he heard Firestorm whinny at an approaching rider. He looked up to see Chloe, her blond ponytail bouncing behind her as she trotted over to where he'd tied his horse.

He couldn't say that he was surprised. A natural caretaker like her was probably worried that he might overdo it.

"You come out to check on me?" he asked.

"No, I was more concerned about the time of day. It's been four hours since you had anything to eat. I figured your hunger pains would be out of control by now."

"Well, what do you know? The woman is not only beautiful, she's smart." He watched the blush creep up her face before she dismounted and turned to dig in the saddlebags.

Was she trying to hide her flush from him? Had she planned to bring more than lunch?

If so, that was a bad idea—although an intriguing one.

"I don't want to get in your way," she said. "I can just leave your food here."

"Did you already eat?" he asked, his gloved hand still gripping a strand of barbed wire.

"No, not yet."

"Then if you'll give me a few minutes, I'll be finished here, and we can have lunch together. That is, assuming you packed enough food for two."

"Are you kidding?" She shot him an impish grin. "I've seen you eat, so I packed enough food for six."

He liked watching her blush, but he enjoyed her witty banter even more.

As he finished pulling the wire around the post, he asked, "You get much done this morning?"

"Actually, I did. I called Teresa's attorney and left a message with him. Then I tackled some paperwork and paid some bills. I'm trying my best to hold everything together until I know what's going to happen with the ranch."

The stress of Dave's death and the pending what-ifs must have been bugging her. And he was glad she was finally opening up to him about it—even if he couldn't help her solve her problems. He wondered where she would go if she had to leave the Rocking C.

Before he could ask, she changed the subject. "It

looks like you know what you're doing." She nodded toward the repaired fence.

"Yeah, who would have known?" He straightened and checked over his work. Then he placed his tools in his saddlebags. "This is my third repair this morning, and each time, it was like second nature."

She stroked Firestorm's nose. "How're you doing on this valiant steed?"

"I must be doing all right. My legs haven't begun to bow. And I'm not sore yet."

She laughed. "That's sounds like a good sign to me."

"So where should we eat?" he asked.

"Up by that copse of trees. There's a little pond there. I believe ranch folk would call it a swimming hole."

Joe froze, and a vision of the pond burst forth in his mind, even though they'd yet to reach it.

As they led the horses around a big boulder, he said, "I've been here before."

"Where?"

"*Here*. This place," he said, unable to mask the awe in his voice.

When they reached a big tree near the water's edge and they tied the horses to one of the low branches, he was sure of it. "I've even swam in that pond."

"When?"

"I don't know. I'm guessing a while ago. Maybe when I was a kid." He scanned the pond that was surrounded by cottonwoods, as well as a tall eucalyptus. "Other things on this ranch have given me a slightly familiar feeling, but nothing like this. I remember this exact swimming hole."

"What else do you remember?"

Joe paced the water's edge as if that would help him go back in time, to relive the moment.

"There used to be a rope swing over there." He pointed at the huge eucalyptus. "It was sweltering hot that day. Dave and I were taking turns launching ourselves off the rope and into the water."

"So you remember Dave."

"Yes. Sort of. We'd been out riding and repairing fence lines, I think. Don't you see? I'd had this uncanny feeling that I'd done that before, too."

"That's great. What else?"

"Dave asked if I knew how to swim. He said, 'I've never seen your aunt or uncle take you guys to the community pool.'"

"Who were your aunt and uncle?"

"I have no idea. I can only remember him asking me that question."

"And he said 'you guys,' like maybe your siblings or cousins or someone else who lived with you."

Joe wanted to recall the exact memory before he examined every detail for clues. So he didn't answer as he walked closer to the eucalyptus. He looked up at the sturdy branch overhead. The swing was gone now, but the frayed end of the rope was still there. "I remember Dave tying the rope up there."

"How old were you?"

"High school age, I guess. Dave slipped and landed in that shallow part right there." Joe pointed to the spot, where reeds still grew out of the water. "He busted his arm, and Mr. Cummings flipped out because we were playing around when we were supposed to be working. So he cut the rope."

"As a punishment?"

"No, I think he cut it down because Dave got hurt on the swing. Dave yelled at his dad and accused him of being too protective."

"Teresa used to say that Dave had a sensitive nature, and that his father used to coddle him at times." Chloe stared off into the distance.

Joe suspected there was more to the story than that. Of course, judging by how secretive Chloe had been while digging around in the desk yesterday, he had a feeling there was a lot she hadn't shared with him about Dave, his parents and the ranch.

If she wasn't going to open up with him, then he wouldn't disclose the rest of his memory with her—including what Old Man Cummings had told Dave while scolding him. The words, the hurt they'd inflicted, rang clear in his mind now.

I knew letting that boy hang out on the ranch was a bad idea, Davey. Joey's a bad influence on you.

The father and son had argued some more, but the rest was too blurry to recall.

Yet the sharp pricks of shame cut just as deeply, the sting just as intense, as if the conversation had unfolded only seconds ago.

And that was the real reason Joe hadn't wanted to enlighten Chloe about that part of the memory. He didn't want her to think Mr. Cummings had been right.

As Chloe unbuckled a rolled up quilt from the back of Rosabelle's saddle and spread it out on the grass, Joe again looked up at the discarded remnant of rope still hanging in the tree and replayed the scene over again in his mind.

He'd been right. He knew Dave before the guy had ever enlisted, which meant they'd gone to high school together. Could Joe actually be from Brighton Valley? Was this small town his home?

No, it couldn't be. Not any longer. He had no dependents, no family. And his driver's license as well as his discharge papers said his home was in California.

He also had a friend in El Paso. Of course, a lot of good that contact information had been. Joe had called him yesterday after dinner. But the man hadn't answered his phone, and he'd let his messages pile up until there was no room left for another one.

Chloe must've been thinking along the same line because she said, "I wonder if we should call Sheriff Hollister and let him know about this breakthrough. Since you can't go into town yourself, maybe he can ask around and see if anyone remembers you."

"I would think that he already asked all the locals that question and came up blank." Joe helped her unpack the bags that held their lunch and carry them to the blanket.

She set out four sandwiches, some leftover scones, a thermos of lemonade and two apples. Then her motions stalled. "You know, if you went to high school with Dave, Sheriff Hollister might be able to talk to some of the other kids who were in your class."

"Sure, but Hollister seems like a smart guy. I'll bet he's already asked every person my age if they remember me. And he didn't have anything to report."

"You have a point. But he did say that he was still investigating."

Joe reached for a sandwich, removed it from the plastic baggie and took a bite, which would help to quench his hunger for lunch. But it wouldn't do much when he was starving for more details on his background.

The small flashback triggered a desperate need to find out more about who he'd been, where he'd been. Even though Chloe was keeping mum about her own business, Joe couldn't keep his memories locked up tight. He needed someone with whom he could bounce off his ideas and theories, and he suspected that the pretty blonde lounging next to him was eager to speculate with him.

"Maybe I was just hired help," Joe said, "like Tomas. That day that we went swimming was hot. And I was here working. So it's possible that the Cummings gave me a summer job, and that I'm not from around here."

"But Dave mentioned your aunt and uncle, so maybe he knew them. You might have only lived with them during summers."

"Then why didn't I list them as my next of kin on my enlistment paperwork?"

They went around and around, speculating and eating and speculating some more. But none of the scenarios they came up with felt right.

Joe was just about to reach for a scone when he decided not to ruin a nice day spent with Chloe by bringing up all the what-ifs. So he lay back on the quilt instead, letting his hat fall off and stacking his hands under his head.

"You know what?" he asked. "As much as I want all the answers right this second, they're not going to magically appear just because we've talked the possibilities to death. I'm just going to have to be patient and hope that something else comes along and jogs my memory."

"Dr. Nielson suggested you give your brain time to heal and let nature take its course. You might only get snippets of memory here and there, but with time, it should all come back to you."

"I hope so."

"It's amazing how you took one look at this pond and *poof.*" She snapped her fingers. "A boyhood recollection reappeared. I wonder what else you can remember by experiencing something similar."

"I wouldn't mind remembering how it felt to lie down under the blue sky and kiss a beautiful woman."

She caught his gaze, and her smile faded. "Is that something you've experienced before?"

"I don't know. Come a little closer and help me find out."

He'd just been testing her, teasing her. But when she smiled, he turned to his side, reached for her and…just let nature take its course.

Chapter Nine

Chloe had no business kissing Joe again, but as those amazing blue eyes reached deep inside of her, as his arms slipped around her and he drew her close, she couldn't help leaning toward him and just...letting go.

She expected the kiss to start slowly—much like the first one had. But the moment their lips met, hers parted, and the kiss exploded with passion.

As their tongues touched, twisting and mating, their hands stroked, explored, caressed.

She knew she should pull back and stop things before they got out of hand, but it had been so long since she'd lost herself in a man's arms, in his kiss.

Then again, her only experience had never been like this. Before she was blinded by a haze of lust and found herself making love outdoors, she drew her mouth from his. She meant to explain her reason for stopping, but she didn't dare say a word until her breathing slowed to a normal rate and her heart stopped pounding.

"That was some kiss," he said.

It certainly was.

"I don't mean to be a tease," she finally said, "but I don't think we should jump into anything."

He ran his knuckles along her cheek. "Because of my amnesia?"

That was one reason to be cautious. She hardly knew the man as it was. And while her heart—not to mention, her body—seemed to insist it didn't matter, that she could easily fall for him anyway, she had to be reasonable.

"Don't you think we should take things slow until your memory returns?" she said.

"Probably."

She bit down on her bottom lip, pondering how much to share with him about the mistake she'd made, but there was a part of her that didn't want him to think she was flighty or that she didn't have any morals.

"I made a bad choice once, and I told myself I'd be more careful next time."

"What happened?"

She really hadn't told anyone before, other than Teresa, but it seemed as though Joe deserved an explanation. "I was lonely and got caught up in a relationship that wasn't right for me."

She'd met Mark Foster her first semester at the junior college in Wexler. She hadn't had a chance to make any friends in town yet, and he'd been funny and charming. She'd been flattered by his interest in her, thinking that he actually cared for her.

He'd pursued her, coming on pretty strong, and she hadn't been experienced in the ways of the world. She should have taken the time to think things through, to get to know his true character, but she hadn't. He'd taken advantage of her naivety by taking her out to an expensive dinner in Wexler, pulling out all the romantic stops and plying her with enough champagne to make her head spin.

She'd never in a million years thought that she'd have

sex in the back of a car—especially her first time. She'd cried afterward. And then she'd gotten sick. The whole thing was a disappointing and embarrassing experience she'd like to forget.

Apparently, Mark had more luck at forgetting than she had. He never called her again, while she couldn't get that awful night out of her mind.

"So what did he do to you?" Joe asked. "Did he break your heart?"

No, it was her self-respect that had suffered the most, which was why Chloe had never shared the embarrassing details with anyone.

"My heart was a little bruised," she said, "but not broken. Let's just say that things didn't work out the way I'd hoped."

She'd learned a hard lesson that night, one that didn't need repeating. From then on, she'd resolved not to drink on a date and not to have sex with someone she didn't love—or barely knew.

And even though she felt as though she could fall for Joe, he had amnesia, and she didn't know any more about him than he knew about himself.

After that heated kiss by the pond earlier that afternoon, Joe had been careful to respect Chloe's wishes, even though it had taken every ounce of his resolve to put some distance between them once he'd come in for dinner.

He was bone tired after a hard day's work, and the hot shower he'd taken upon entering the house had refreshed him only enough to eat the chicken and roasted potatoes Chloe had made for dinner. When his eyes began drifting closed at the table, his little Florence Nightingale returned and ordered him to bed.

Within minutes of his head hitting the pillow, he'd fallen into a deep sleep, and his dreams took him far away from horses and watering holes, from two laughing boys and an irate rancher.

As Dave's father's words grew dim, the vision's backdrop shifted from a green and fertile Texas ranch to a dry and dusty urban war zone in Afghanistan, where bullets flew and mortar boomed...

Three or four Taliban insurgents carrying assault rifles and strategically hiding in an abandoned apartment building fired on Joe and his men. And they took cover behind an overturned minibus.

"Hold your positions," Joe commanded.

His communications specialist had radioed for backup. He just needed to keep his troops in cover position a few more seconds until reinforcement arrived.

The metal tracks of the cavalry tank sounded, just a short distance away, providing a sense of relief. But the corporal beside him fidgeted with his rifle, clearly on edge from more than just the gunshots around them.

"I can't take this no more," the corporal said, tears streaming down his face. "If she doesn't want me, then what do I have left?"

"Hold tight, buddy. The armored tanks are almost—"

Before Joe could finish his order, the young marine was up and running, revealing their hid-

ing position and exposing the other members of their patrol squad.

"Fall back, Dave. Fall back!" Joe screamed. But the hotheaded corporal didn't listen. Instead, he charged toward the snipers, spraying bullets at no target in particular.

Dave only had so many rounds, and when he emptied his rifle, he'd be a sitting duck. As the squad commander, Joe was responsible for all of his men, even those who were hell-bent on disobeying direct orders and compromising the safety of fellow marines.

"I'm going after Corporal Cummings," Joe told the man beside him. "Cover me, but don't move until the armored vehicles set up a block-ade. On three..."

Joe ran out to Dave, grabbed the crazed man by his pack and pulled his body back toward the safety of the minibus. But his friend swung his rifle around, clocking Joe in the face, allowing the snipers above them to get a free shot.

Dave, weighted down by his full gear and a rage of helplessness, fell onto Joe just as the first lumbering Humvee pulled in front of them. But not before Joe's knee exploded.

"Dammit," Joe yelled. "I told you to fall back, Dave."

A tap on his shoulder, followed by a gentle hand tugging at him, drew him out of the gunfire, the dust and the heat.

"Joe, wake up. You're having another nightmare."

At the sound of Chloe's voice, he almost lurched out

of bed, determined to dive over her body and protect her from enemy fire. But her calming strokes along his biceps told him that she was real, not just a figment of his nocturnal imagination.

"Here," she said, "have some water."

He sat up, letting the sheet drop to his waist, and took a deep drink from the glass she offered him.

"Sorry for being such a…" What? A head case? A nut job? He shook his head and sighed. "I'm sorry for waking you up. *Again*."

"Don't worry about it," she said, her words coming out softly, soothing him.

Just having Chloe near helped. His racing pulse slowed, but his pounding heart wasn't so quick to respond.

"You went through a traumatic ordeal," she said, "and it's only natural that you'd dream about it."

Was she talking about the accident that had robbed him of his memory? Or the battle he'd just relived in his sleep?

He let out a deep breath and ran his hand through his hair before taking another gulp of water.

"Do you want to tell me about it?" she asked as her fingers continued their soothing caress along his upper arm.

She was wearing a thin cotton nightgown, the hem barely reaching her thighs when she sat beside him on the bed. She meant to comfort him, no doubt, but his decelerating heartbeat leaped back into action, quickening its tempo.

He'd tried so hard to be a gentleman earlier tonight. To keep his distance so he wouldn't be tempted to pull her into his arms for another heated kiss like the one they'd shared on that picnic blanket.

In the dim light filtering in from the hallway, he could see her expression and realized it was one of concern, not lust. So he didn't dare meet her eyes. Not when his thoughts had shifted from the war zone to the bedroom.

He lowered his gaze to her chest, where the clinging cotton gown she wore couldn't hide her rounded breasts. She wasn't wearing a bra, and as her arm moved up and down so she could rub his biceps, he could see the outline of her dusky nipples with each movement.

"Another dream?" she asked.

"It was the same as before, only more detailed. I think it was a memory of the battle I read about in Danielson's report."

Her hand shifted from his side to his back, and with each stroke of her fingers along his spine, his arousal grew. If he couldn't get his hormones under control, he'd have to get her off his bed and out the door before he did something they'd both regret later.

Amnesia or not, he was still a man. And if she kept touching his bare skin like that...

"I'm okay now," he said. "Go on back to bed. You need your rest, too."

"You're still shivering. I'm not going to leave until your body settles down."

Oh, yeah? If she kept stroking him like that, taunting him, his body would never calm down. He wasn't shivering because of his nightmare. Just looking at her tousled hair and sleepy eyes had riled him up.

Unable to take it anymore, he grabbed her hand, his fingers circling her wrist.

Her mouth opened slightly in surprise, but she didn't try to pull away.

"Listen, Chloe. If you don't get back to your room right this second, I'm going to do a lot more than kiss you."

The pulse in her wrist quickened, and her eyes dropped to the sheet barely covering his lap. His arousal had to be obvious.

She raised her gaze to his, but she didn't make a move to leave.

He continued to hold her wrist, his thumb tracing slow circles on her skin. Their gazes met and locked. He lifted his free hand and cupped her jaw. Yet she didn't seem to be the least bit worried about what might happen if she continued to stay with him.

He leaned forward and brushed his lips across hers— gently, just in case she came to her senses and decided to pull away.

Instead, she opened her mouth, allowing his tongue to explore her warm depths. She pressed in, her own tongue matching his with equal fervor. He pulled her closer, her breasts splayed against his bare torso.

He was tempted to tear the thin fabric so he could feel all of her warm fragrant skin against his. He needed the intimacy, the closeness of another person.

No, not just any person. He needed *Chloe*.

He drew back slightly, trying to read her expression, to gauge her thoughts.

Her eyes, glazed with passion, searched his face, too, as if trying to assess what he might be thinking, feeling.

"Are you sure?" he whispered, loud enough to appease his conscience, yet soft enough for her to realize she had the power to slow things down or bring them to a complete halt.

She reached for the back of his neck, drew his mouth to hers and whispered against his lips, "I'm sure."

They kissed again, long and deep. As his hands slid along the bare curve of her back and down the slope of her hips, a surge of desire shot clean through him. He lifted the hem of her nightgown and removed the barrier before laying her down beside him.

He paused a moment to drink in the angelic sight of pretty Chloe, lying on his bed. Her throat flushed, her lips plump from their kisses.

"You're beautiful," he said.

A slow smile stretched across her lips. "So are you."

He didn't know about that. He was beat up from a hard day's work and scarred from battle—and who knew what else. But her words pleased him.

Her nails skimmed across his chest, sending a shimmy of heat through his blood, and he kissed her again until they were both drowning in need.

She pulled her lips from his, yet she continued to hold him. "I want to feel you inside me, Joe."

Words he'd been hoping—maybe longing—to hear.

As she opened for him, he entered her. She raised her hips to meet him, and their bodies became one, taking and giving.

As they both reached a peak, he released with her, and their climax set off a sexual explosion that left him seeing stars.

The night stood still, and nothing mattered but the two of them and what they'd just experienced in each other's arms. That is, until reality settled over him.

He had nothing to offer her. At least, not until his

memory returned. So he hoped she wouldn't consider this another mistake she'd made, or him to be another bad choice.

While he was tempted to tell her that she was safe with him, another more pressing, more daunting reality slammed into him.

He'd been so caught up in desire that he'd neglected to even consider using any means of protection.

Did he dare mention that to her? Had the thought even crossed her mind?

He stroked the length of her arm, then took her hand in his. "As nice as that was, as much as I enjoyed it, we got a little carried away. We didn't use any protection."

"I know," she said a bit breathlessly. "I just realized that."

He gave her fingers a gentle squeeze. "I'm not an irresponsible lover. It's just that…"

"I know," she said again. Then she smiled. "I don't think we have to worry about pregnancy. It's not the right time of the month. But we'll need to plan ahead next time."

Thank goodness. He was relieved that she wasn't too worried. And glad that she'd said "next time."

He blew out the breath he'd been holding, then drew her close, wrapping his arms around her.

Still, his momentary relief and gladness couldn't block out the regret that began to settle over him.

His body was in the most relaxed state of bliss it had been in as long as he could…well, at least since he woke up in that hospital bed. But his mind was still reeling. And the dream Chloe's presence had chased away thirty minutes ago came back to haunt him once again.

In that nocturnal window to the past, Dave had been

talking about a woman right before he'd made a suicidal run straight into enemy fire. A woman Joe suspected was Chloe.

If she doesn't want me, then what do I have left?

Had Dave really said that? Or was Joe's spotty recollection once again playing tricks on him?

What exactly had been between Chloe and Dave? She said they were only family friends, but what if Dave had believed they were more than that?

The woman dozing softly beside him felt perfect in his arms. But nothing else felt right. Not even his name. Who in the hell was Joe Wilcox? And what was he doing on the Cummings ranch, living Dave's life?

Joe was staying in the man's house, sleeping in his bed, riding his horse. Had he just slept with Dave's lover, the blonde who'd driven him to risk death over life without her?

If so, Joe had no right to any of it.

As Chloe stretched her arms over her head, she listened to the sound of running water coming from the bathroom down the hall.

She should be mortified that she'd woken up naked in Joe's bed, but thinking about the way he'd brought her body to life last night, she felt nothing but contentment.

Still, she couldn't just lay here and bask in the memory. She should get up and get dressed before Tomas arrived for work.

Instead, she pulled the sheet tighter around her and snuggled deeper into the mattress.

Why didn't she feel any remorse for her behavior last night? For enjoying their lovemaking so much that she was hoping Joe would get out of the shower and come back to bed?

When she'd hurried into his room to waken him from his nightmare, he'd given her several opportunities to leave. Yet, despite what her mind had told her, she hadn't been able to get her traitorous body to follow suit.

She had no job and, once the attorney started probate on the ranch, she would have no home. In short, she had absolutely no future. On top of that, she had no idea who Joe really was or where he'd be going once he regained his memory.

So then why was she smiling and frolicking with a stranger in bed as though she had nothing to lose?

The sound of an approaching pickup—the foreman, no doubt—reminded her that there was work to be done today. And that she still had a reputation to uphold, even if her stay on the Rocking C was only temporary.

She sat up and spotted her nightgown on the floor across the room, lying right where Joe had tossed it.

Joe. How would he act toward her this morning? He was usually so lighthearted and playful—never taking things too seriously. Maybe some of his attitude was rubbing off on her because she didn't much feel like taking any of this seriously, either.

If she did, it might hurt too much when it was all over.

She crossed the hall to her bedroom, her steps faltering. Maybe there was plenty to regret. They'd made love without protection last night. And while it was a fairly safe time of the month, accidental pregnancies occurred.

While she showered and shampooed her hair, she tried to shake off the remote possibility—and the fact that she'd been reckless again last night. Not that she regretted what she'd shared with Joe. That part had been amazing. But she should have considered using a contraceptive.

After drying off with a fluffy towel, she slipped on a pair of jeans and a white blouse. She topped it off with the only Christmasy thing she could find—a red sweater. By the time she entered the kitchen, Joe already had the coffee made. He stood at the counter, cracking eggs into a bowl. A steaming cup of java rested within his reach.

She smiled to herself as she thought of the appetite he must've worked up last night.

"Good morning," she said, the softness in her voice revealing more vulnerability than she'd had when she woke this morning.

"Hey, you're up. Good. Breakfast is almost ready."

She told herself not to look too deeply into his eyes for hidden messages. But maybe she shouldn't bother. Reading men didn't seem to be her forte. At least, not in the past. So she decided to just go along with the flow.

"I see you're cooking again," she said.

"It's the least I can do after keeping you up so late last night."

A blush warmed her cheeks, and while she headed for the coffeepot, she avoided eye contact. She reached into the cupboard and removed a mug. Then she filled it with the fresh morning brew, adding a splash of cream and a spoonful of sugar.

"Just for the record, I didn't mind waking up in the middle of the night." She smiled, then lifted her cup and took a sip.

Their brief morning-after banter was cut off by a rapping on the back door.

It was Tomas standing on the porch, his hat off, his brow furrowed, his expression laden with worry. "Hurry, Miss Chloe. It's Lola. She's going to foal, but something's wrong."

"Did you call the vet?" Chloe asked, her mug quickly forgotten on the counter.

"Yes, but Dr. Peterson's answering service said he was on vacation. Another doctor is handling his patients while he's gone. They gave me his number."

Chloe followed the foreman to the barn, Joe close on their heels.

"Were they going to contact the other vet?" she asked. "Or should we do that?"

"He's just down the road at the Beecham ranch. The woman at the answering service said she would call him on his cell, but the reception isn't very good there. Maybe I should just drive over and get him myself. It'll be faster."

Poor Tomas. Chloe's heart went out to him. He was a good man and a hard worker, but he hadn't wanted the foreman position. He was good with the animals, though. And he was obviously worried about the mare he'd been babying for her entire pregnancy.

"Okay," Chloe said, "you go get the doctor. I'll stay out here with Lola and try to keep her calm."

Tomas nodded, then hurried from the barn, presumably to his own truck, which was more reliable than Ol' Greenie.

"You okay?" Joe asked.

Chloe hoped her own worry wasn't reflected in her eyes because Joe looked concerned enough for both of them. One thing she'd learned early on in her work with patients was to keep the family members calm.

"Yes, I'm fine. The Beecham ranch is only about ten minutes from here, so the vet should be here soon enough."

"Do you have much experience with horses and breech births?"

"Honestly, I don't have much practice with any type of births. Horse, breech or otherwise. I've always specialized in geriatric care. Not too many labors happen at the Sheltering Arms."

Joe stepped away from Lola and placed a hand on Chloe's shoulder. "Relax. I'm sure she'll be okay."

All the stress that Chloe should have been dealing with this morning as she lounged around in his bed rushed into her heart, and reality grew as big as Lola's belly.

"But what if Lola isn't all right? She's our prize mare. That foal she's carrying is worth thousands. We bred her with Night Wind, a stud from Houston who's sired plenty of prize cutting horses. The Rocking C has a lot riding on this birth being a healthy one."

"What happens to the ranch if Lola can't pay her way?"

"The whole place could go under." She blew out a ragged sigh, revealing the truth she struggled with each day. "I've tried my best to run things since Teresa died, but I'm a nurse, not a rancher. Now that Dave's gone, who knows what will happen to the place?"

And more worrisome of all, who knew what would happen to Chloe?

Chapter Ten

So the Rocking C was in limbo.

Joe suspected that Chloe wasn't only concerned with the bottom line or the ranch's finances. From the sound of things, he sensed that she was also concerned about herself. What would happen to her if she had to move?

He knew she wasn't selfish. Didn't he? At least, nothing she'd done up until now would make him think so. In fact, it was just the opposite. Yet something nagged at him, something he couldn't put his finger on.

It was probably a side effect of the amnesia.

"So what would you do if you could stay on the ranch?" He'd meant the question to distract her from worry. At least, that's what he told himself. But had he been fishing for ulterior motives?

And if so, why?

His question seemed to hang in the air for a moment, then she said, "I don't know. I've had a few ideas. But like I said, I'm not really a rancher, I'm a nurse. There aren't too many jobs that would incorporate the two."

"Tell me some of them."

She bit her bottom lip, but before she could answer, a pickup drove into the yard and parked.

"Oh, good," she said, her voice light as she shook

off his question altogether and strode toward the black Dodge Ram. "That must be the vet."

Joe watched a dark-haired man slide out of the driver's seat. The moment the vet looked up, his blue eyes zeroed in on Joe, and recognition dawned on him like the noonday sun.

Joe had a feeling he knew the guy, too. It wasn't a flashback coming to him in the same way one struck him out by the swimming hole. This was different.

Maybe it was the blue eyes, the dark hair and the olive complexion, because the vet was as familiar to Joe as the face he saw in the mirror each morning.

"Oh, my God," the vet said. "*Joey?* Is that you?"

Joe wasn't sure what to say. Nor did he know how much he wanted to divulge about who he thought he was or what his circumstances were. But Joe wanted answers more than anonymity.

As the vet eased closer, Joe said, "Yeah."

"It's me," the vet said. "Rick."

Joe was almost too stunned to speak. Had he recognized the guy because he'd actually known him in the past? Or because of their resemblance and the fact that Rick the vet had called him Joey?

"Do you know Joe Wilcox?" Chloe asked the vet.

He had to, Joe thought. They looked similar enough to be brothers.

Brothers? The moment the word crossed his mind, a flicker exploded in his brain, illuminating a couple of the dark corners that had been hidden.

This guy—or rather, Rick—had been a part of Joe's life at one time. But he'd be damned if he knew any more than that.

"I've been looking for you for almost ten years." Rick

started to reach out toward Joe, possibly to pull him in for a brotherly hug. But then his movements stalled, as if he thought better of it. He ran a hand through his hair instead and slowly shook his head. "Have you been on the Cummings ranch all this time? I never realized you and Dave were so tight."

Chloe coughed discreetly, and Rick glanced her way as if he'd forgotten she was standing there, watching the awkward, one-sided reunion.

"I'm sorry." Rick reached out to shake the extended hand Chloe offered. "I'm Rick Martinez, and I haven't seen my brother since we were teenagers."

Joe couldn't do much more than stand there, staring at the man who looked just like him and claimed to be his long lost brother. This amnesia crap was getting to be too damn much for him.

"But Joe's last name is Wilcox," Chloe said, looking only slightly less confused than Joe felt.

Rick turned to Joe, his brow furrowed, his head cocked slightly. "What'd you do? Change your name? Maybe that's why Clay Jenkins couldn't find you."

Clay Jenkins. The computer guru? Joe had been right. He really had recognized the billionaire's photo—and not necessarily because he'd seen his face in magazines or newspapers or online.

But those few little dots were the only ones his brain would let him connect.

Damn. Joe hated not having an answer to questions like that. And he was sick and tired of repeating the same mantra time and time again. But he didn't have any truthful options. "I'm afraid I don't know."

The furrow in Rick's brow deepened, and Chloe jumped to the rescue once again. "Joe was hit by a car outside the Stagecoach Inn and suffered a head injury. He has amnesia, so we're not exactly sure who he is."

Before Rick could respond, Tomas jogged out of the barn and interrupted. "Doctor, please. Lola is this way. She needs you."

"Of course." Rick squared his shoulders and grabbed a case out of the back of his truck before following Tomas into the stable.

Joe watched his brother walk away. He might have stood there gaping like an idiot, but Chloe elbowed him to get his attention.

When he glanced down at the petite blonde's up-turned face, she arched a single brow and nodded toward the barn. "Do you remember him?"

"I...I don't know. I mean, he looks just like me. And even though we have different names, there definitely seemed to be something there when I saw him. Not necessarily an immediate fraternal bond, but *something*."

Chloe hesitated for a minute. "Let's go into the barn. Maybe seeing Dr. Martinez in action or spending some more time with him will trigger another memory."

Joe followed her, feeling like a lost little child who needed direction.

Up until this point, he hadn't let the amnesia render him helpless, and he wasn't about to start now. This was his first major opportunity to learn more about himself. And he needed to face it head on.

When they reached Lola's stall, Rick was already examining the mare. "You were right, Tomas. The foal is breech."

Lola whinnied, and Rick stroked her neck and made soft shushing sounds. "It's okay, mama. It's okay."

Joe could almost believe him. Maybe things would soon be "okay" with him, too.

Joe hung out in the barn until Lola had dropped a healthy foal—a filly. Then he'd gone to the kitchen to put on a pot of coffee. He figured Rick would want to talk to him, and it seemed like a better idea to do it while seated at the kitchen table and not out in the driveway.

The pot had just stopped percolating when Rick entered the kitchen from the mudroom.

"How's Lola doing?" Joe asked.

"Happy to have it all over, I'm sure. But she and her foal are bonding, so that's good. Tomas and Chloe are with her now."

"How about some coffee?" he asked.

"Sounds good. Thanks."

As Joe poured two cups of the fresh brew, he said, "So, you're my brother."

"It's been ten years, and you've grown up—and filled out. But I believe you are—unless you're an amazing lookalike."

"You believe it—or you *know* it? I mean, if you haven't seen me since I was sixteen, how can you be sure?"

The vet hooked his thumbs into the front pockets of his jeans and studied him quietly—and not at all defensive that Joe was calling him out to prove his claim.

"You have a three-inch scar on your right arm," Rick said. "A burn mark you got when you were eight. Tío Ramon, our uncle, came home, cocked and ready for a fight. When Tía Rosa didn't get dinner on the table fast enough, he grabbed the frying pan off the stove. It had hot oil in it because she was getting ready to fry corn tortillas, but Ramon didn't give that a second thought. He threw it at her, and you jumped in front of her to protect her and got hit instead."

Joe closed his eyes, the truth setting in, even if the memory hadn't surfaced. Then he rolled up his right sleeve and showed Rick the raised scar...

As Rick reached out and fingered the scar, another vision flashed in Joe's brain, this one involving a ten-year-old boy, a younger version of Rick, rubbing ice along the same strip of singed flesh on a smaller arm—Joe's arm?—and saying, *You'll be okay. But stay out of Tío's way next time he comes home drunk. You and me gotta stick together.*

"So," Rick said, intruding on Joe's flashback, "you joined the Marines. That would make sense. You were always trying to protect people—Tía Rosa, kids being bullied at school."

"You told me that the two of us had to stick together," Joe said, but not accusingly. He was just sharing a memory.

"I tried, Joey. I really did."

Maybe so, but they'd obviously had some kind of falling out. Otherwise, Joe would have given Rick's name and address as a contact number.

"So what happened?" he asked. "Why didn't we stay together?"

"After they arrested Tío Ramon and protective services got involved, we were sent to different foster homes. Then, about the time I turned eighteen, Mallory got pregnant, her grandparents sent her out of state and my life spiraled out of control for a while. You ran away and it was damn near impossible to find you—

even with the help of a private investigator and a computer whiz."

"Who's Mallory?" Joe had no more than asked the question when Chloe entered the kitchen, her hair falling loose around her shoulders, clearly worn out from the ordeal with Lola—and most likely, their own late night.

Rick glanced at her as though he wasn't sure how to answer any personal questions in front of a nonfamily member, then returned his focus on Joe.

But hell, Joe wasn't sure he wanted her to know all the details, either. It sounded as if they'd had a pretty crappy life. And from what Chloe had told him, her childhood had been picture-perfect.

Besides that, he had this inexplicable urge to keep some stuff private—between him and his brother.

Sure, Chloe had taken excellent care of him after the accident. He'd been completely dependent upon her and, after last night, their relationship had only gotten stronger.

So why did he feel the need to hide things from her? And why did he question whether he could fully trust her?

Judging by the questioning look Rick was directing at him, Joe didn't think his brother trusted her much, either. But when Joe didn't object, he said, "Mallory is my wife now. But back in high school, she was my girlfriend. She got pregnant, and…well, things got pretty complicated. Let's just say that I had a lot on my plate back then and was too young to do much about anything."

"You mentioned Clay Jenkins had been looking for me, too. Do I know him?"

"You, Clay and I ran around together in high school. He has a computer business now. And after I got my DVM degree and was in a position to find you and take care of you, I started looking for you. When I continued to run into walls, probably because of your name change, I finally called him and asked for his help."

"So I'm from Brighton Valley originally?"

"Wow, you really don't remember much of anything." Rick turned to Chloe, directing the question at her. "How long has he been like this?"

Joe bristled. It was almost as if Rick thought Joe was too simpleminded to answer for himself.

"Nearly a week." Chloe looked at Joe as if wanting to get his permission to continue.

He nodded, and she went on to tell Rick about the accident and everything else they'd found out from NCIS since then. But Joe tuned them out, as another flashback popped into his mind, one of a teenage Rick telling Joe he needed to get a hold of his temper. *Don't be such a hard-ass, Joey. If you get sent to juvie, I can't take care of you there.*

Joe was so absorbed in his own thoughts and flickering memories, he almost didn't catch the fact that Chloe hadn't mentioned Dave or his letter.

"So what were you doing in town in the first place?" Rick asked him. "Do you remember that?"

"No, they tell me that I had a letter from Dave Cummings in my pocket when they found me. According to military records, I served with him in the Marine Corps before we both got medically discharged."

Joe told Rick about Dave's death and hoped his brother didn't ask what was in the dying man's last letter. Because the truth was, Joe had no idea himself, since that was another thing that Chloe had yet to tell him.

Maybe that's why he didn't completely trust her.

Rick's cell phone rang, and Joe wanted to throw the offending object into the yard. Didn't the answering service realize that the vet had just found his long lost brother, and they had years to catch up on?

Rick looked at the screen and then silenced the phone before saying, "Listen, I know this is probably a lot for you to take in. And Lord knows that I want to spend the next two weeks out here with you catching up and helping you figure things out. But I don't want to overwhelm you, and I promised Doc Peterson that I'd take care of his emergency calls while he's on vacation. I'd like to stop back tomorrow so I can check on Lola anyway."

"I'd like that," Joe said.

"All right. I'll see you then."

Joe wasn't sure if he should shake Rick's hand, but his brother made the decision for him and pulled him into a tight squeeze, giving him a few solid thumps on the back. "Man, I missed you, Joey. We'll have to play catch-up tomorrow."

Joe was reluctant to let go, but he still had all his ranch chores to take care of and a lot of thinking to do. So he walked Rick out to his truck. All the while, he started a mental list of things to ask his brother.

As Rick got into his truck, Joe watched him drive away.

His life was finally coming together. He had a brother, a family. And his memory was slowly coming back, albeit in scattered pieces.

So why did he still feel unsettled—as if he still had unfinished business?

* * *

After Dr. Martinez left and Joe went to help Tomas with the chores, Chloe sat at the kitchen table, staring into her empty coffee mug. She didn't know what to make of it all. Joe's discovery that he'd grown up in Brighton Valley and that he had a brother had been mind-boggling. But what effect—if any—would that have on their budding relationship?

There hadn't been any of the awkwardness she would have expected after they'd slept together, since they'd barely had a chance to touch upon it this morning. The foal's birth had interrupted their conversation, making it easy to avoid asking him, "Now what? Where do we go from here?"

Then Dr. Martinez had provided another diversion when he'd arrived with his surprising revelation.

Chloe found the news almost overwhelming and couldn't begin to imagine how Joe must feel.

Just moments ago, he'd asked her to call Sheriff Hollister and relay the recent development, which was probably because he was still trying to wrap his mind around it and wasn't ready to talk about his thoughts.

So, using the kitchen phone, she dialed the sheriff's office. When he answered, Chloe filled him in.

"Well, what do you know," Sheriff Hollister said. "But I wonder why my deputy didn't find any links to that family tie of Joe's when he was going through high school yearbooks."

"From what Dr. Martinez said, Joe must have changed his name to Wilcox after he left town."

"Is that right? Hold on a sec." The sheriff's voice drifted when his mouth no longer spoke directly into the receiver. "Taylor, bring me those Brighton Valley High yearbooks you were looking through." After an unmistakable rustle of pages, the sheriff continued, "Yep, I found him. Joseph Martinez. He's a sophomore here, just a kid, but I'm sure that's him."

"Joe came to town to deliver Dave's letter," Chloe said. "But maybe he planned to get reacquainted with his brother while he was here."

"That would be my guess. He rented that car for two weeks, so that would certainly give him time for a visit."

She sure hoped that was the case. From what she'd gathered, Joe and Rick had been estranged after a falling-out—a bad one. Otherwise, Joe wouldn't have left town, changed his name and not contacted Rick for ten years.

The fact that he might be the kind of man to hold a grudge was a real possibility. And if so, that wasn't an admirable trait. Had she jumped into a sexual relationship too quickly? It certainly wouldn't be the first time.

But last night had been so very different from her only other experience. It had not only been amazing, but it had been special. And, at least on her part, it had been a decision of the heart.

"By the way," Sheriff Hollister said, "I was going to call him and let him know that we received an anonymous tip. One of the customers at the Stagecoach Inn drives a vehicle that matches the description of the one that hit him. We're still investigating, so we haven't made an arrest, but with that information, coupled with Joe's apparent connection to Brighton Valley, I seriously doubt that he was a targeted victim. So he doesn't need to keep hiding out on the ranch anymore."

"It's okay for him to go into town?"

"I'm sure it's fine."

"He'll be glad to hear that." And while Chloe took it as good news, too, she couldn't say that she was especially happy that Joe was free to leave. Sure, she was relieved to know that no one was out to get him. And it warmed her heart to know that he had at least one family member who obviously loved him—and a local, upstanding citizen at that. But still, at the same time, she found it unsettling.

She'd known there would come a time when he would go back to his old life, but what about the new one he'd just begun to create with her?

"If anything comes up," Sheriff Hollister said, "or if we make an arrest, I'll let you know."

"Thanks. Joe will appreciate that."

Chloe had no more than ended the call when the subject of her thoughts walked into the kitchen and provided her with a brand-new dilemma.

Should she tell him that he was free to leave, that there was no need for him to stay cooped up on the Rocking C any longer? Or did she dare to keep the new information to herself so she could hold on to him a little longer?

Was there really even a choice?

"I came to get some water to take with me out to the pasture," Joe said, as he hung his hat on the peg near the mudroom door.

She watched him proceed to the cupboard for an insulated jug. Then he carried it to the kitchen sink and turned on the spigot.

While he filled his container with water, she said, "I just got off the phone with Sheriff Hollister." She went on to relate everything the lawman had told her.

"So I'm free to venture off the ranch now and head into Brighton Valley? I can actually leave?"

"That's what he said. But if you're not feeling up to it—or if you like being here—you're welcome to stay as long as you want to." She bit down on her lower lip, hoping he'd tell her that he didn't want to go. That he'd come to…care for her. And, that after last night, he… might even love…

That possibility was almost too wild to imagine, although she'd felt her feelings drifting in that direction.

"I'd like to take a look around town," he said. "It might spark more memories. But if it's all the same to you, I'd feel more comfortable staying here on the ranch for a while."

Chloe released the breath she'd been holding, but she reined in her enthusiasm. "I think that's a good idea."

"So what do you have planned for this afternoon?" he asked.

"I'm going to drive out to the nursing home. I'd like to visit Sam Darnell and ask him a few questions about ranching. But I can wait until you're finished helping Tomas. That way, you can come with me—if you want to. And when we're done, we can drive down Main Street. Maybe we can even go to the ice-cream shop near town square."

He seemed to give the idea some thought before shaking his head. "I'd better pass. Tomas has a lot of work to do, and I know he'd appreciate my help. Maybe we can go into town next weekend."

Chloe wondered if Joe was trying to avoid being with her or if he was reluctant to bombard his brain with too many memories all at once. But she hated to confront the issue head-on right now. They'd probably both feel better about discussing it later this evening—before bed, when it would be impossible to avoid asking him what their next step should be.

Ten minutes later, after changing her clothes, she grabbed her purse, climbed into Ol' Greenie and drove to the Sheltering Arms.

She stopped in the lobby, where Christmas music played softly in the background—the toe-tapping tune of "Jingle Bell Rock." She took a moment to appreciate the holiday decor and the faint scent of pine. Then she continued on her way to the elevator, humming along with the spunky beat and thinking that December was, indeed, a "swell time."

When the doors opened, she rode up to the third floor, where Merrilee Turner was manning the nurse's desk again. She smiled when she spotted Chloe. "You're back. It's good to see you."

"Thanks. I stopped by to visit Sam and Ethel."

"Sam is in his room, watching TV. But Ethel is probably sleeping. At least, she was the last time I stopped by her room. She's picked up a cold and has a nasty cough."

"That's too bad. Does Sarah know?"

"I mentioned it to her, and she said she'd put a call in to the doctor."

"That's good." Chloe just hoped Sarah hadn't forgotten. The woman was often scattered and forgetful—not a good trait for the third-floor nurse to have. But she had other habits and traits that Chloe found even more troublesome.

When Chloe had worked at the Stagecoach Inn, she'd often seen Sarah partying with her friends and throwing back quite a few beers, keeping late hours on nights when she was supposed to be at work early the next day. It wasn't like she would call in sick, but she'd often come in late and hungover. And she had a tendency to snap at the aides, as well as the patients.

But since Merrilee was the one who'd picked up on Ethel's illness, at least it had been noted. So Chloe wouldn't stress too much about it.

"If Ethel is resting," Chloe said, "I'll let her have a few more minutes to sleep."

"Good idea."

Chloe's first stop was Sam Darnell's room, where the retired cowboy lay in bed, his head propped up with pillows, his lunch still on the portable bedside table.

"Hey," she said, peering at the food he'd yet to touch. "What are you doing? Having a late meal?"

"Nope. I'm done. They just haven't come in to haul the dishes away."

"But you've hardly eaten a thing."

"I wasn't hungry. A fella doesn't burn up too many calories when he's laid up in bed."

She glanced at an untouched slice of three-layer cake with gooey frosting. "I can't believe you didn't eat your dessert. You love chocolate. And you never sent sweets back to the kitchen when I worked here."

"That's because you used to force me to eat, and I didn't have the heart or the energy to wrestle with you."

Chloe laughed. "I did no such thing."

They made small talk for a while, then Chloe told him about the offer she'd received for the hundred head of cattle.

Sam clucked his tongue. "Don't take it. That price is way too low. The guy might as well come onto the ranch in the middle of the night and rustle the entire herd."

"I had a feeling he was trying to take advantage of me."

"A lot of folks will do just that if you don't stand up for yourself."

Sam had said as much to her before, so she gave him the same response. "You know that I don't really like confrontations."

"But sometimes you gotta stand up for what's right."

"I know. And I will." After a beat, she added, "I don't suppose you'd come out to the Rocking C with me and negotiate that deal."

Sam brightened. "I'd be happy to. But do you think you can spring me from this place?"

Chloe crossed her arms. "I'm not sure. Do you think you can eat your lunch?"

"You drive a hard bargain, missy. How 'bout I just eat that cake?"

Chloe laughed. "Are you sure you don't want to come out of retirement? The Rocking C could sure use your help. And I could, too."

Sam let out a harrumph, but his tired eyes sparked and glistened in a way she hadn't seen since his wife passed away.

"You don't want me," he said. "I'll be eighty-two on my next birthday. You'd be better off with a younger man."

"I already have one. But Tomas told me himself that he's not foreman material, and while I like him a lot, I'd have to agree. Besides, I need someone who's savvy about things like this, someone I can trust."

He seemed to consider her suggestion. "I couldn't give you a full day's work anymore, but I wouldn't mind coming out to the ranch and having a little look-see.

And I'd actually like to talk to that cattle buyer. I'd let him know that he ain't messing with a fool greenhorn."

Chloe smiled. "I'd like that, Sam. Let me see what I can do about getting you out of here in the next day or so."

"Call my nephew. He'll give the okay. He's also a fancy city lawyer who likes to throw his weight around."

"I'll do that." Chloe watched Sam dig into the cake. And when he'd swallowed the last bite, he chugged down his milk.

Maybe all he needed was to feel useful again. She'd have to keep that in mind.

After saying goodbye and promising to come back, she headed down the hall to check on Ethel, only to find the frail, silver-haired lady dozing, the blankets pulled up to her chest.

Her arms were uncovered, her hands at her side. She wore a long sleeve flannel gown, but her wrists were in plain sight—and completely bare.

Apparently her allergy alert bracelet, which was supposed to be on order, hadn't come in yet.

Not wanting to disturb her dear friend, especially if she was sick and needed her rest, Chloe remained in the doorway a minute longer. Then she turned away and left the room.

As she walked to the elevator, she spotted Sarah Poston at the nurse's desk, standing over Merrilee and complaining about something.

"I take it that Ethel's allergy alert bracelet hasn't come in," Chloe said.

Sarah crossed her arms and shifted her weight to one foot. "It should be here any day. Besides, like I told you, her allergy is noted in her chart."

If Chloe still worked here, she'd peek at Ethel's chart herself. But she'd been let go, terminated unfairly for speaking her mind about Sarah's disregard for protocol and her attitude toward certain patients.

Too bad Ethel didn't have a family to insist that she get the best quality care possible. For a couple of beats, Chloe considered her options at this point.

One came to the forefront. *Sometimes you gotta stand up for what's right.*

Yes, but how far did she want to go in challenging Sarah? Did she want to take it up with the administrator—again?

She really didn't have any solid evidence against the woman. Was she prepared for the fallout if her accusation didn't prove true?

Chloe hated confrontations, especially those she didn't think she could win. Besides, there was another confrontation awaiting her at home—one she was dreading, but one that had to be faced.

Because she and Joe needed to talk about the sexual turn their relationship had taken last night.

Chapter Eleven

Throughout the day, while working with Tomas, Joe's memories continued to return sporadically and in no particular order.

Sometimes he'd get a vision, a brief glimpse into the past. At other times a feeling would wash over him—a righteous anger or just plain sadness—which only frustrated him more.

At first, he'd assumed that he'd been angered or hurt by something his brother had done. And that's why he'd left town and never looked back. What else would have compelled him to change his name and lose contact with his family?

Yet each time he'd looked at Rick yesterday, he'd sensed a strong brotherly bond. And while he was more than okay with that, he couldn't just accept everything at face value.

Even more troubling was the fact that, in spite of his life slowly coming back to him, he still didn't have a handle on his true identity, either, and that left him more unsettled than ever.

For that reason, after dinner, he thanked Chloe for the meal and turned in early, giving himself a chance to sort through the mixed-up feelings alone.

She was so understanding about it, too. Which confused him all the more. Most women would want to know why the man they'd spent the previous night with all of a sudden wanted to sleep alone. But not Nurse Chloe.

He rose early the next morning, when he was sure she'd still be asleep. Then he went outside to check on Lola and her foal. There'd been plenty of chores to do, so he kept himself busy until Rick arrived.

Joe greeted his brother in the yard, then walked with him to the barn, where Rick examined Lola and the foal.

"They both look good," Rick said.

Joe thought so, too. "I checked on them earlier this morning. Lola sure seems to be a good mother."

Rick glanced at his boots, then back to Joe. "You and I weren't so lucky."

"Somehow, that doesn't surprise me."

"Do you remember any of it? That apartment complex where we lived? The fighting? Dad running off with that stripper? He'd said she was a professional dancer, but I didn't buy it. And neither did Mom."

"I have a vague recollection, but nothing solid."

"What about moving in with our aunt and uncle after Mom died and Dad took off? Do you remember that?"

"Last night, when I undressed for bed, I noticed that scar on my arm. You'd told me what happened, but I was able to remember it—the yelling and screaming. The huge sense of relief I felt when the police arrived before our uncle beat the crap out of her. The feeling that it hadn't been the first nor the last time something like that had happened."

"Things were pretty bad at times. I don't blame you for wanting to put it all behind you. I might have run off, too, but Mallory had been sent to Boston to finish out her pregnancy and have our baby. And I'd wanted to wait for her to come back. Then I met up with Hank Lazarro, who helped me turn my life around."

Joe wondered if he'd found a mentor of his own along the way. Had Conway, the retired marine, stepped in and befriended him? Had Joe gone on to find new friends and a family in the corps? The answers to his questions seemed to be yes.

"Hey," Rick said, placing a hand on Joe's shoulder. "Why don't you ride into town with me? I've been craving Caroline's hotcakes all week. And since I left home early this morning, I didn't get a chance to have breakfast. We can talk in my truck and at the diner. Maybe that will jostle your memory."

Joe had no idea who Caroline was or what diner his brother was talking about, but he'd slipped out of the house without eating, too. "That sounds good to me."

Twenty minutes later, they entered the small town eatery, where a middle-age waitress, a woman Rick addressed as Margie, greeted them with a smile. "Good mornin', Doc Martinez. Who have you got here? Don't tell me this is Joey, all grown up."

"Yep. It sure is."

"Where've you been, son? We haven't seen you in… well, it's been ages."

"He joined the Marines after he left town," Rick said. "And when I went off to college, we lost touch for a while."

Apparently, Rick hadn't told anyone Joe had run off.

"Isn't that nice? Y'all found each other. And just in time for Christmas." Margie grabbed a couple of menus and led them back to a corner booth, all the while chattering about how family should be together during the holidays.

When she offered them menus, Rick said, "I don't need one. I'll have the rancher's breakfast—eggs over easy, bacon and a stack of Caroline's hotcakes."

"I'll have the same thing," Joe said, "only with scrambled eggs and the country sausage."

"Coffee?" Margie asked, as she made a note of their orders on a small pad.

"You bet," Rick said. "Thanks."

When Margie walked away, leaving the brothers alone, Rick said, "Neither one of us had the kind of past I liked to talk about, so very few people around here know anything about where you went or why." He reached into his shirt pocket and pulled out some snapshots, one black-and-white, the others in color. "I brought some family pictures for you to see. I thought it might help."

When he handed them over, Joe looked at each one, then focused on the old Polaroid of a couple in their late twenties to early thirties.

"That's one of the only shots I have of our mom and dad," Rick said. "You can see that she's blonde. We obviously get one of our genes for blue eyes from the Norwegian side of the family."

Joe wished he could say that he remembered their parents, but he didn't. "How old were we when mom died?"

"You were six. I was eight."

At that age, Joe doubted that he'd have too many memories of them anyway. He flipped through the pictures and found one of a dark-haired couple in their mid-forties. He flashed it at Rick. "Is this Ramon and Rosa?"

"Yeah. Do you remember them?"

"Vaguely, but more than I remember our parents. I keep getting flashes of memory—bits and pieces I'm trying to put together. So keep talking. I think it's working."

"Tío Ramon was Dad's brother. He liked to stop by La Cantina, a little dive in Wexler, every night after work. He was a mean drunk and had some anger issues, especially when he was three sheets to the wind. I'm sure that had a lot to do with him not keeping a job. But for some reason, he always seemed to find a new one."

"You mentioned the abuse, the domestic violence. It must have been pretty bad."

"It was. Ramon and Rosa loved each other, but they fought something awful, especially when they'd both been drinking."

Margie stopped by with the carafe of coffee and filled both cups. Then she left a creamer and sugar.

Rick thanked her, and when she walked away, he continued. "We'd tried to talk Rosa into leaving him before it was too late, but she didn't listen. And one night, he nearly killed her. After Ramon went to prison and Rosa recovered from that last beating, she joined AA and turned her life around. She and I reestablished a relationship, although we weren't especially close at first. I've since reconciled with Tío Ramon, too. But that's been fairly recent. I wanted to be sure that he was serious about his sobriety. And I believe he is. He's due to get his two-year token next spring."

Joe lifted his mug and took a sip. "I'd think he could use some anger management classes."

"That was mandated by the court. He took them while he was in prison, but he took a refresher course after his release. He and Tía Rosa have reconciled and are attending church regularly. You'd hardly know them."

Joe hardly knew them as it was. And something told him he ought to be grateful that he'd forgotten those early years.

Rick took a sip of coffee. "Because Tío kept losing his job, it seemed as though we had to move each time he found a new one. We lived in several different apartments in Houston, a mobile home and a duplex in Wexler, and then a townhome in Brighton Valley. After I met Mallory in my junior year, I spent more and more time away from home. And that left you to deal with all the family dysfunction on your own. I think you felt abandoned, and I can see why you would. I'd like to say that I wasn't much more than a kid at that time, but I won't make excuses. I was all you really had, and I let you down."

Joe forgave him. At least, the man he'd become after the accident did. And maybe the old Joe did, too. After a ten-year separation, a tour of duty in a war zone, and an accident that damn near killed him and left him with amnesia...well, he was glad to have someone and something to hang on to. And that someone was sitting across the table from him, looking at him with eyes laden with emotion.

"I love you," Rick said. "And I missed you something awful. Now that we've both grown up and moved on, I'd like to establish a better relationship."

"I'd like that," Joe said. "I'd like it a lot."

Margie returned to the table and placed their meals in front of them. Just a whiff of the sausage triggered another memory. Joe paused, allowing it to unfold.

Seated at the kitchen table, Joe watched Tía frying breakfast meat, her bruised eyes nearly swollen shut, her bottom lip split. The words Joe said to her that morning. *You gotta leave him, Tía!*

I know, mijo. *But deep inside, your* tío *is a good man. And I love him.*

But next time, he could kill you. And me...

The memory faded. And while it really wasn't a whole lot for Joe to go on, it validated the things Rick had told him.

Yet that simple vision and the feelings it triggered stirred up even more bits and pieces, allowing him to cobble some of them together.

"You're right," Joe said. "I felt abandoned and left alone to weather the storms at home. I remember trying to talk some sense into Tía Rosa. I'd beg her to leave him, but she wouldn't listen. It used to make me so angry because it wasn't just her life she was ruining, it was mine. I'm not sure that she even cared that each time I stepped in to protect her, I'd get beat on myself."

"I should have been there to protect you."

Joe shrugged a single shoulder. "Maybe, but I wasn't looking for protection as much as a backup. If you'd have been home one of those nights, we could have stopped him and knocked some sense into him."

"You're probably right. But in retrospect, that might have landed you and me in juvenile hall—or worse."

Joe reached for his fork, only to have another memory kick in, one that he'd never forget again. And along with it, more emotions: anger, frustration, grief.

"What's the matter?" Rick asked. "Did you remember something else?"

"Yeah. Going home after what must have been their

last fight. Red lights were flashing all around the neighborhood. The sheriff was there. Not Hollister, but an older man—heavyset, graying hair. He had *Tío* cuffed and locked in the back of the squad car. *Tía* was already in an ambulance, and they wouldn't let me see her."

"She nearly died that night. She spent two weeks in ICU and nearly six months in rehab."

"I remember thinking that it was all my fault," Joe said.

"There's no way. You weren't even there when it happened. *Tío* was a brute when he drank."

"Yeah, but if I'd been home, I might have stopped it."

Rick reached across the table and placed his hand over Joe's. "You were only fifteen. And if you *had* been there, you would have tried to stop it. But then you might have been the one hauled off in the ambulance or the squad car."

"Maybe so."

Joe didn't bring it up because he didn't think it was necessary, but he also remembered that he and his brother had both been sent to different foster homes that night, separating them when Joe had needed him most.

"I can't fix what happened in the past," Rick said. "But I want you to know that I'm sorry for whatever I might have done to you—or whatever I failed to do for you. You're my brother, and I don't want you to leave town without knowing how I feel."

"Speaking of leaving Brighton Valley," Joe said, "do you have any idea why I might have changed my name after I left?"

"I can't be sure, but I think it was because you wanted to put our lousy past behind you. Ramon and Rosa made newspaper headlines for a while, and the whole mess was pretty embarrassing. I found it hard to deal with and didn't speak to either of them for years. But Ramon learned a hard lesson while he was incarcerated. You might find this hard to believe—I know I did—but now that he's quit drinking and gone through some intensive counseling, he's like a new person."

Joe wished he had something to say to that, some feelings to go along with it, but he dug into his breakfast and let his scattered thoughts and memories simmer.

By the time they'd finished eating, a lot of things had begun to come together for him.

The foster parents Joe had to live with weren't too bad, but Darrell, one of the other kids, used to bully the smaller boys. And since Joe had seen more than his share of abuse—and hated it—they butted heads more often than not.

One day, when Darrell began picking on one of the band geeks in the school cafeteria, Joe confronted him. A fight broke out, and even though Joe's reason for getting involved was noble, the principal suspended them both.

Rick hadn't been around that day, which led Joe to think he'd probably ditched school to spend time with his friends. And more than ever, Joe began to feel helpless and alone—with no one to care about him.

He had, however, earned the undying support of the band geek he'd stepped in to help—Dave Cummings.

Pieces of his ranch memories began to come together, and Joe soon realized when he'd been on the Rocking C before.

On several occasions, he'd run away from home and had ended up on the Cummings ranch. Just being around Dave and his parents had given him a glimpse of what a real family was supposed to be like, and he'd found himself drawn there.

"Do you need to go back to the ranch now?" Rick asked as he pushed his plate aside. "If not, I can take you to my place and you can meet Mallory and our son, Lucas. I can't wait to introduce you."

"I guess I should head back to the ranch. Maybe when my head is on a little straighter, I'll make a better impression on your wife and son." Joe really wasn't up to meeting anyone right now, especially with his thoughts and feelings still jumbled. But it was nice that Rick had asked.

Joe took one last look at the picture of his parents, trying to get another vision, another memory, but nothing came to mind.

He handed the photos back to his brother. "I'm glad I can't remember how crappy life was before our mom died."

"She had a prescription drug problem, which eventually killed her. She died of an overdose."

A vision slammed into Joe, striking him as hard and unexpected as the Silverado pickup that had hit him in the dead of night, causing his amnesia in the first place.

Overdose.

Dave, cold and lifeless, sprawled out on the kitchen floor. The pain meds he used to swallow—two and three at a time, washed down by whatever liquid was handy.

Bits and pieces of his memory merged with the disjointed dreams he'd had, unleashing a storm of emotion: Worry and disappointment, irritation and resentment.

And it all came back to him.

Well, not all of it. But the memories of a battlefield

will... Joe blinked, remembering Dave giving it to him, as well as the message Dave had asked Joe to deliver on his death and the reckless, suicidal rush at the Taliban insurgents... They were still a bit scattered, but they were clues enough.

He finally understood why he'd returned to Brighton Valley in the first place. He'd promised Dave he would deliver that letter, which Chloe hadn't let him read.

The annoyance he'd felt off and on since the accident rose up inside of him, bordering on anger. And a sense of betrayal lanced his heart.

Dave had loved that woman enough to give her everything. And she'd led him on, convincing him that she loved him, too. Then she'd dumped him, and Dave had chosen death over life without her.

Just like Joe's mom had done when she hadn't been able to cope after their dad abandoned his family for that stripper.

More distrust and suspicion crept over him as another vision, this one recent, flashed before him: Chloe in the Cummings den, digging through files and scanning papers.

She'd looked up and spotted him in the doorway, guilt splashed across her face.

Her reaction had left him uneasy at the time, and now he knew why. He hadn't trusted her.

But why? What clues had he missed? He racked his brain, trying to recall things she'd said to him when they'd talked about the Rocking C.

As the fragments of their conversations came back to him, he tried to make sense of them.

I'm trying my best to hold everything together until I know what's going to happen with the ranch.

Had she already known about Dave's death before the sheriff had notified her? Joe had, but that memory had been lost with all the rest.

I don't want to move until the new owner is located.

Joe had quizzed her about that at the time. *The new owner?*

Whoever stands to inherit the ranch now that Dave is gone.

Chloe had given him the impression that she planned to move on. Yet she seemed to have settled in at the Rocking C, even going so far as to decorate the house for Christmas.

Joe had asked if she'd like a ranch of her own, and if so, would she give up her plan to go to nursing school.

I don't know. Maybe. I'd probably invite some friends to live with me, so I'm not sure how much time I'd have to study.

Damn. Did she already have plans to take over the Rocking C? Would she fill it with friends and free-loaders?

I'd like to visit Sam Darnell, a retired cowboy I know, and ask him a few questions about ranching.

So she did mean to stay on and to make a go of the place. Apparently, she'd planned to all along. And when Joe had seen her in the den, rifling through the files, she must have been looking for a will or a deed or something that would secure her claim.

His gut twisted as suspicion settled over him. He shifted in his seat, but was unable to shake it.

What had that last letter said? Had Dave told her what he'd planned to do—and that he'd left her the ranch?

"Are you okay?" Rick asked. "You look a little shaken and confused."

Was it that obvious?

Joe blew out a sigh. "I've just had a major break-through, Rick. Things are still a little sketchy, but images and memories are slamming into me, along with a slew of emotions I'm trying to deal with. And the more I think about it, the less comfortable I feel about staying at the ranch. Would you mind taking me back for my things, then dropping me off at the Night Owl?"

"I'll take you anywhere you want to go. But if you're looking for a place to stay, come home with me. Mallory and I have a guest room, and you're more than welcome to stay with us as long as you'd like. Besides, I want you to meet Lucas. He's a great kid—and the spitting image of you."

Joe had been a loner most of his adult life, but he didn't want to be alone tonight. "If you're sure Mallory won't mind."

"She's eager to meet you—and she'll be glad to have you with us, especially for Christmas." Rick reached into his pocket and pulled out his car keys. "But why don't you just drop me off at the clinic and take my truck to pick up your stuff from the ranch?"

Joe took the keys, while Rick picked up the check. "Thanks. It won't take me long to pack."

"Keep the truck as long as you need it."

Joe didn't expect to be more than a few minutes at the ranch, just long enough to talk to Chloe. And to say the words he'd meant to have with her when he'd first crossed city limits.

Chloe was seated in the kitchen, staring out the bay window, when she saw Dr. Martinez's truck pull in the driveway. She knew Joe would be returning soon, but she hadn't expected to see him behind the wheel.

That was odd. She couldn't imagine a busy veterinarian like Rick not needing his vehicle, which meant Joe must not be planning to stay long.

Oh, for Pete's sake. What was wrong with her? The man hadn't even entered the house and she was already reading way too much into the situation. But one look at the scowl marring his face, and she knew something wasn't right before he even made it to the back porch.

She met him at the mudroom door, just as he let himself in. Before she could quiz him about driving his brother's truck, he said, "I came to pick up my stuff."

"What? Why?" She followed him to the guest room, hating herself for morphing into the kind of woman who got all clingy when a man was trying to leave. But she deserved to know just what in the heck was going on.

He pulled open the dresser drawers and piled his new pants and shirts on the bed.

"What are you doing?"

"I'm getting my things."

"Why?"

He turned to her, his eyes full of something she'd never seen in his expression before. Disgust? Blame? Anger?

"I had a major breakthrough while I was at Caroline's Diner with my brother."

That should have been a good thing, but why was he so…cold?

"A big chunk of my memory came flooding back almost all at once, and I finally remembered the real reason I came to Brighton Valley in the first place." He scanned the room, his gaze landing on the clothes he'd placed on the bed, then he raked his hand through his hair. "Dammit, I don't even have a freakin' suitcase."

"I can get you a bag—if you need it." She still didn't understand why he wanted to leave.

"I probably should have just left all of this here, anyway. It's not like I'm going to need any ranch clothes any time soon. Unlike you, who'll apparently get everything your scheming heart had hoped for."

What was he talking about?

And just who did he think he was talking to?

"Slow down, Joe. What in the world is going on?"

He tore his gaze from the folded clothing, from the bed where they'd so recently made love and zeroed in on her. "I'm talking about what you did to Dave. How you convinced the poor guy to leave everything to you. And then you dumped him, right when he needed you most."

"What?" Chloe crossed her arms. "I didn't convince Dave of anything."

"Right. Well, that's not how he figured it. He was crazy in love with you, and you broke his heart. Hell, the truth of the matter is, you broke *him*."

Chloe closed her eyes, Joe's words echoing the guilt that she felt since learning about Dave's death. For the briefest of moments she wanted to turn away in shame, but she shook off the misplaced feelings.

"Listen, Joe. It wasn't like that with me and Dave. We never had anything together. We certainly never had…" She waved her hand between the two of their bodies. "We never had this."

"This?" Joe gazed at her, his expression accusing her all over again.

But she held firm. Dave hadn't been emotionally stable, and she hadn't done anything wrong.

"What we had wasn't…" Joe's voice trailed off, and his expression softened. Then he sat on the bed, shoulders slumped.

The nurse in her was ready to forgive him for lashing out at her when his memories still had to be a jumbled up mess. But the woman who'd given him her heart was crushed.

"What we *had?*" she asked.

"Hell, I don't know. Had. Have. I won't deny that I fell for you, but I can't very well stay out here with you knowing now what I should have known all along."

"And what's that, Joe? What *do* you know? Please clue me in, because you seem to suddenly have all the answers, and I can't even begin to understand why you're so angry—especially at me."

"I don't know. Maybe because Dave was one of my men—and a buddy. And I knew how damn much he loved you, idolized you. And maybe because I crossed a code of honor between friends."

"Dave only *thought* he was in love with me. He was upset over his mom's illness and death and he latched on to me and mistook the friendship I offered him. But I assure you, it was only friendship on my side. I never lied to him or misled him. In fact, I even sent him a letter explaining as clearly as I could that nothing romantic would ever happen between us."

"Yeah." Joe leaned forward, placed his elbows on his knees and held his head as if to shake loose his thoughts—or maybe to hold them still. "I saw what that letter did to his psyche. Hell, what it did to his whole career. Crap, what it did to *my* whole career. Your so-called 'clear explanation' caused him to lose it when we were under attack." He looked up, caught her gaze. "You know my nightmare?"

Chloe said nothing, not wanting to be reminded of their passionate lovemaking that had followed that same frightening dream. Not when he'd just practically accused her of killing Dave herself.

"It all came back to me. Before running into the gunfire, Dave told me he couldn't go on without you. So, yes, I'm familiar with that carefully worded letter you sent him."

She felt compelled to ease closer, to sit next to him on the bed, but her wounded pride wouldn't have been able to recover if he got up or moved away. So she stood firm and tried to reason with him. "If you remember Dave's words and his recklessness, then surely you must know how sensitive he was. How he didn't handle things very well. I'm sorry that he's dead, and I'm sorry that your knee and your career are blown. But those were a result of Dave's actions, not mine."

He blew out a ragged breath, but he held his thoughts at bay.

"Was I supposed to lie to him and let him think there was something between us? Do you think I should have promised to be waiting for him when he came home from war?"

Joe gazed up at her, his eyes filled with accusation. "But you *were* waiting for him. You even told me that you were taking care of the place for him. Or maybe you were just taking care of your own investment, banking on Dave's fragile mental state to secure you a ranch of your own."

He couldn't have shocked her more, hurt her more, if he'd struck her with his fist.

"What are you talking about?" she asked. "I've wasted months of my life holding this place together because I promised his mom, not him, that I would. How would his death in any way benefit me?"

"Because Dave signed a battlefield will right before he died leaving the entire ranch to you."

Chloe almost sunk to the floor. Her hand, which trembled with indignation only seconds ago, flew to her mouth, which was incapable of speech anyway.

Joe's expression held no warmth, no familiarity. "That's why I came to Brighton Valley. To deliver my buddy's letter and to see for myself just what kind of woman would take a poor sucker like him for everything he had."

"Are you kidding me? I can't believe that you think me capable of that. How could I…? How could *you*, especially after we…?" She didn't know what she was trying to say, but she was too stunned to continue.

"If my memory had been intact, nothing would've happened two nights ago."

Now even the compassionate nurse in her let sympathy and understanding go by the wayside. His accusations were so far-fetched. But still, she could only handle so much confrontation, and it didn't look like there was anything she could say to change his mind. And right this minute, her pride didn't want her to even try. So she stayed silent, fuming with indignation.

"I'll be staying at my brother's house for a while, at least until I can wrap my head around everything." He got to his feet and reached for the folded clothes. "But don't worry. I won't interfere with the probate or bother you anymore."

And with his parting shot striking her heart dead

center, cracking it right in two, he walked out of the room, out of the house and out of her life.

She wasn't sure how long she continued to stand in the bedroom that had once held sweet memories of their lovemaking. She was too busy reeling from his hurtful words, from his false accusations, to form a solid game plan.

Yet in spite of her pain and disappointment, she felt a sense of peace, too. When Joe had blamed her for causing Dave's depression and, ultimately, his death—something for which she'd also blamed herself—she'd stood up to those charges, rejecting them and defending herself. And by doing so, she was able to release the guilt that had once tormented her and accept the truth.

Dave had been devastated by the loss of his mother and by his decision to join the Marines when he should have been home trying to mend his relationship with his father. He'd also felt somehow to blame for his dad's heart attack—or at least for the estrangement that had shortened what little time on earth they'd had together.

His guilt and conflicting duty to family and country, as well as the battlefield itself, must have taken a toll on him, and Chloe refused to accept responsibility for his death.

But that didn't mean she wasn't crushed by Joe's other allegations, by his lack of faith and trust in her.

It took every ounce of strength she possessed to not fall onto the bed, curl up into a ball and cry her eyes out. But once he was long gone, she gradually moved from the disbelief and bargaining stage to anger.

How dare he accuse her of setting her designs on Dave or on this ranch?

She might not like confrontations, but she wasn't

about to take this lying down. So she went to the den, plopped down in the desk chair and picked up the phone. Teresa's attorney hadn't returned her call yet, but she wasn't going to wait for him to find time to get back to her. If she had to track him down at his home or in the courthouse, she'd do it.

Luckily, Mr. McDougall's secretary said he was in the office and transferred her call right away.

"Hello, Ms. Dawson. I got your message, but things have been pretty hectic this morning. What can I do for you?"

She explained about Dave's death and about requesting the documents from the San Diego coroner's office.

"Okay. As soon as I get that report, we can get the ball rolling and settle the estate."

"That leads me to another issue, Mr. McDougall." Chloe didn't know how to word her question without sounding like the gold digger Joe had accused her of being. But there was no other way to get the answer she needed. "What exactly is going to happen to the estate?"

"Did Dave have a will?" the attorney asked. "I never made one for him."

Chloe told him about the handwritten will he'd made in Afghanistan, which may have listed her as the heir. "But I don't know if it's legal. Actually, I don't even know if it exists. I haven't seen it."

"Well, if he did have one—and you can find it— probate will go more smoothly. From what I remember, the Cummings family didn't have any other relatives or people who could lay claim to the ranch. So if the will exists—and if it's legit—then you'd be the owner of the Rocking C."

Great. Chloe didn't want the burden or the guilt

that would come along with that sort of unexpected inheritance.

"On a side note," the attorney said, "I do have a copy of Dave's life insurance policy—the one he took out before his last deployment. It names Joseph Wilcox as the beneficiary."

If Chloe hadn't already been seated in the old desk chair, she would have fallen to the floor. "Joe Wilcox is the beneficiary?"

"Yes. Do you know him?"

"Not as well as I thought I did. But I know where you can find him." Chloe provided the attorney with Rick Martinez's contact information.

They made an appointment to meet in person, then ended the call.

Chloe would sure like to see the look on Joe's face when he learned that Chloe wasn't the only person who benefitted from Dave's death. It would serve him right to have to eat his words.

She supposed that was cruel to think something like that at a time like this. But she was still furious with Joe for breaking her heart and crushing her dreams. And she was also angry at Dave for putting her in this situation to start with.

She'd never asked for any of this.

Yet, here she sat.

Out the window, she spotted a squad car pulling into the drive. So she headed for the front door, just as Sheriff Hollister knocked.

The sheriff stood on the porch, holding two green canvas duffel bags, both of which appeared to be military issued.

"Afternoon, Miss Dawson. The clerk over at the

Night Owl called us and let us know that they found these bags in the room Joe had checked into. Apparently, they were wedged under the bed. My deputy must have missed them in his initial search of the room."

"Why are there two?"

"One appears to be Joe's. The other is probably Dave's. Is Joe here?"

"Uh, no. He's at his brother's right now." Chloe should probably tell Sheriff Hollister that Joe had moved out, but she wasn't ready to explain why or what had happened between them.

"Should I bring them inside for you?"

No. She didn't want anything more to do with Joe, Dave or their stuff.

"Just leave them on the porch," she said. "I'll make sure that Joe gets them."

Chapter Twelve

Chloe didn't want to hold on to those duffel bags any longer than she had to. So after the sheriff left, she lugged them to Ol' Greenie, one at a time, then heaved them into the back.

After returning to the house to get her purse and to lock up, she climbed into the truck and drove to Rick's veterinary clinic since she had no idea where he lived.

But when she pulled into the parking lot, which was nearly empty, she spotted Rick's truck.

Apparently, this was where Joe had holed up. Well, she'd just leave the bags with him and be done with it.

Better yet, she'd tell him he could just come outside and get the fool things himself. So she headed for the entrance to the clinic and stepped into the waiting room.

The moment Joe spotted her, he got to his feet. She felt like lighting into him, but she didn't see the use. "Sheriff Hollister stopped by with two duffel bags. I told him that I'd give them to you. They're in the back of the pickup."

His expression softened a bit. "Listen, Chloe. I'm sorry if I might have come across a little harsh."

She stiffened. "A *little* harsh? You were a complete jerk."

He raked a hand through his hair. "I didn't mean to

jump you the moment I entered the house. It just happened. All the memories and bottled emotions erupted. And I should have at least thanked you for what you did for me. You didn't deserve to get reamed. I just need some time to think things through."

"Take all the time you want," she said. "But first come outside and get those duffel bags."

Before either of them could make a move, her cell phone rang. She glanced at the display. The Sheltering Arms?

"Excuse me. I need to take this."

When she answered, Merrilee said, "Chloe, I'm sorry to bother you, but I thought you'd want to know."

Her heart dropped to the pit of her tummy. Could this day get any worse? "What's wrong?"

"Ethel took a turn for the worse, so I called 9-1-1. Paramedics took her to the Brighton Valley Medical Center."

"Is she okay?"

"No, she's had a complication."

Chloe knew what her friend was going to say before she even said a word. Still, she asked, "What happened?"

"She was diagnosed with pneumonia and given an injection of penicillin. I'm afraid she had a serious allergic reaction, so they sent her to ICU."

"I'll head over to the hospital now. I'm going to ask the nursing staff to see if her allergy was noted in her chart. I bet it wasn't."

"What'll you do if you're right?"

Chloe left Joe standing in his brother's waiting room and headed for the door. "After I talk to Dr. Nielson at the hospital and check on Ethel, I'm going to the Sheltering Arms. It's time I took Sam's advice."

"What'd he say?"

"Sometimes you gotta stand up for what's right."

"What are you going to do? You don't even work here any longer."

"I don't care. If Sarah lied to me about Ethel's allergy being noted in her chart, or if she assumed that it was and didn't double-check to make sure, I'm going to blow the whistle on her, as well as the entire administration for not doing something about my initial complaint sooner."

"I was afraid of losing my job before," Merrilee said. "But I'm not going to stand by and let Sarah risk another patient's life. I'll back you up any way I can."

"Thanks. I'll let you know if there's anything you can do to help."

Chloe was unlocking the driver's door, sliding behind the wheel and turning on Ol' Greenie's ignition before she noticed that Joe had followed her outside.

He might want to talk, but she'd have to deal with him later. In fact, she probably ought to thank him for pumping her full of courage and spunk. Because right now, the normally mild-mannered, former nurse's aide who'd avoided confrontations at all costs was cocked and loaded for bear.

After Chloe drove away, Joe stood in the parking lot, trying to make sense of it all.

He was still standing there, staring in the direction Ol' Greenie had gone, when Rick came out of the clinic. If his brother noticed anything weird about the way Joe was gaping or at the confusion that had to be splashed on his face, he didn't say anything.

"I'm finished here," Rick said. "Let's go home."

"Okay." Joe nodded at the duffel bags resting on the ground. "Let's put these in the back of your truck."

Minutes later, Rick pulled into the drive of a white, two-story house on Chinaberry Lane. After grabbing both bags and the sack of Joe's clothes, they entered the front door.

"Honey," Rick called out, "I'm home."

The words had a nice ring to them, and Joe was happy for his brother.

When a beautiful blonde with an obvious baby bump entered the living room with a warm and welcoming smile, Joe reached out his hand in greeting.

Mallory took it and gave it a gentle squeeze, but instead of letting go, she blessed him with a smile. "Would you mind if I gave you a hug, Joey? You have no idea how happy your brother is to have you back in his life—and how excited I am to have you home in time for Christmas."

As weird and awkward as it might have once seemed to be reunited with people he'd once thought he'd never want to see again, the sincerity in Mallory's gaze made it pretty darn easy to…well, to lower his guard and step into her embrace.

"Thanks, Mallory. I appreciate…having a home where I can…spend the holiday."

"Where's Lucas?" Rick asked.

"He's at Jimmy's," Mallory said. "He'll be back at four. Do you want me to call and ask him to come home now?"

"No, let him play. There's plenty of time to introduce him to his uncle." Rick turned to Joe. "Why don't I show you to your room so you can put that stuff away?"

"Sure." Joe followed his brother upstairs and to the guest room.

"Would you like a soda or iced tea?" Rick asked.

"Maybe later. If you don't mind, I'd like to go through my bag and see what's inside."

"Take your time. I'll be downstairs." When Rick stepped back into the hall, he paused and glanced over his shoulder. "Want me to close the door and give you some privacy?"

"That's not necessary."

Rick had no more than left the room when Joe began to rummage through his bag. When he found a couple of photographs, he paused to look at them.

One was a picture of him, Rick and Clay shooting baskets at the park. That photo must have been taken right before he and Rick had been separated and placed in different foster homes.

The anger that had exploded inside him back at the ranch began to make sense. Only now, it was targeted at the people who'd hurt him the most—his uncle for being a mean drunk, his aunt for allowing her husband to abuse her and the system that had taken him away from the one person who'd always taken care of him.

But he was no longer angry at Rick, as he'd been when he'd first run away. Looking back, as an adult, Joe couldn't blame his brother for wanting to escape their childhood. Or for wanting to create a home with Mallory.

His thoughts drifted to Chloe, to the night he'd held her in his arms after making love. At the time, he'd wanted to create a home for himself, too, a place where he felt like decorating Christmas trees, eating scones and sipping hot cocoa.

But Joe had pretty much ruined any chance of a dream like that happening, especially with Chloe. It hadn't seemed to matter an hour ago, but he wasn't so sure about that now.

Was it Chloe who'd made him yearn for home and hearth? Or was it just being at the Rocking C itself?

When things had escalated at his foster home and then again at school, Joe had made up his mind to run away for good. He'd had enough and wanted to put it all behind him—the embarrassment following his uncle's arrest for domestic violence, the trouble with the principal, the perceived abandonment of his brother.

He had a little money from working on the Rocking C that summer and, instead of purchasing a ticket all the way to L.A., where someone might find him—if anyone cared to look—he purchased tickets for the trek in segments. He traveled first to San Antonio, then to El Paso and on to Albuquerque. He'd intended to end up in Los Angeles.

The only person who knew of his plan—and the only one he'd told goodbye—was Dave, who'd kept his secret as promised.

So at sixteen, Joe left town—and his past—behind him. And he never—well, he rarely—looked back.

He set the photo aside and picked up another, this one taken somewhere in Arizona with the marines who'd become his friends and family.

There'd been a bad accident on the interstate on the final leg of his trip. The marines had been on leave and were returning to their duty assignment in Yuma when they'd pulled up alongside his bus and immediately jumped out and became heroes that day.

Joe had always helped the underdogs, like Dave Cummings and Clay Jenkins, when they'd been bullied in high school. He'd also tried to protect his aunt, only to get battered for his efforts. But when Red Conway, an older marine, actually asked for Joe's assistance, he'd stepped up, of course, gaining respect and hero status in the process.

After the accident, the sergeants were in a hurry to get back to Yuma so they wouldn't be AWOL. But instead of riding with the other passengers on a different bus to Los Angeles, Joe hitched a ride with his new friends. Red offered him a place to stay, and they all took him under wing, each one replacing the big brother he'd once had.

The day he turned eighteen, in an attempt to embrace his future by shedding his past and everything that reminded him of the lost boy he'd once been, Joe began the process to legally change his name. His marine buddies encouraged him to get his GED and to join the corps, helping him set a goal and find a purpose.

Joe set the picture aside and picked up one of him and Dave outfitted in matching camouflage. Dave had followed in Joe's footsteps and enlisted a few years ago.

But in spite of getting through boot camp, Dave had a tough time making the transition from the coddled only son of an overbearing rancher to a marine. So like his buddies had done for him, Joe took Dave under his wing, doing his best to coach him and help when he could.

When he found out that Dave had been assigned to his battalion, he asked Red to pull a few strings, and they managed to get him transferred to the same squad, where Joe could look out for him.

But Dave had never been cut out to be a devil dog. Or a grunt. Chloe had been right when she'd said he was too sensitive.

Joe had always liked the guy, but he could become needy and emotional when things got tough. In fact, Joe remembered wondering what a pretty girl like Chloe saw in Dave. He'd figured money or property had interested her more. And that might have been where his angry, suspicious vibes had originated.

Sure, Dave's family owned a ranch, but if a woman who looked like Chloe had wanted to get her hands on some quick cash, she certainly could have set her sights a lot higher than Dave.

Joe's stomach flopped and his face heated as he thought of the insults he'd flung at her. Had he been so angry at Dave's senseless death, the loss of his career and his promise to return to the one place on earth he'd vowed to never step foot in again that he'd lashed out at the only person he could find to blame?

It seemed that way.

As he recalled how his words had hurt her, his gut twisted hard and tight.

Chloe had taken him in when he was a complete stranger. She'd befriended the elderly patients in the nursing home. And, from what he'd gathered after listening to her side of a telephone conversation, she'd just sped off to become a voice for them.

How had he forgotten all she'd done? How she'd made it fun to trim the tree, decorate the house, eat scones and drink hot cocoa?

And then, when he'd been caught in the throes of a

nightmare that had been more real than imagined, she'd sat on the bed, whispered soothing words, stroked his arm…

He'd fallen for her that night—for the woman she really was and not the woman he'd imagined her to be.

What a heartless fool he'd been.

Joe put his stuff back in his duffel and proceeded to empty out Dave's bag on the guest room bed. Uniforms and street clothes toppled out, as well as a few pieces of mail and a folder. He recognized Chloe's handwriting on one envelope. Joe had seen that letter when he'd packed up Dave's effects and set out on his Brighton Valley trip. But he hadn't wanted to read it then.

He pulled out the folded stationery to see what she'd had to say.

Dear Dave,

I'm sorry that you're far away from home and feeling so lonely. And while I appreciate your kind words, I have no idea where you got the idea that we were even dating, let alone engaged. You're a good man, and I pray each night for your safe return home.

I've taken a break from nursing school so that I can look after the ranch until you get here. I'd promised your mother that I'd do that, and when I make a commitment to someone I care about, I keep it.

But that's the only commitment I've made—to your mother. Once you get home, I'll move into a studio apartment near the junior college in Wexler. I considered waiting to tell you these things to your face, but it seemed that with each letter you wrote, your dream of a future with me grew. And I don't want to give you false hope.

Someday you'll find a woman who truly loves you—and one who deserves you and all you have to offer her.

I hope you understand. In the meantime, please take care of yourself.

Your friend, Chloe

·She'd been right. Her letter had been direct, but gentle and kind. And Dave had made a reckless choice.

What had Joe done?

Chloe hadn't wanted the ranch. Or anything from Dave—certainly not the guilt from his suicide, if that's what he'd actually done. Yet, Joe had accused her of all of that and so much worse.

He needed to see her, talk to her and apologize. How could he have been such an ass?

Before he could shove Dave's stuff back into the bag and head downstairs, Mallory knocked on the doorjamb and poked her head in. "There's a call for you. It's a Mr. McDougall."

She handed him the cordless phone, and he took the call.

"Is this Joe Wilcox?" the man asked.

Joe wondered how he knew where to find him. "Yes, it is."

"I'm the attorney handling David Cummings's estate. I'm not sure if Chloe Dawson mentioned me or told you I would call, but she gave me your contact number."

Chloe had said something about talking to an attorney. At the time, he'd thought that she'd been trying to stake her claim. But in reality, she'd probably been as overwhelmed with the situation as he'd been. And she'd merely wanted to hand over the reins to the ranch and get on with her life.

"She mentioned it," Joe said, "but I don't really know the details."

The attorney spoke of the probate process and filing paperwork as Joe's mind drifted to how he could apologize to Chloe for all of the horrible things he'd said.

What would he do if she refused to forgive him?

"So," McDougall said, "as dual beneficiaries, you might want to consider working together to make a go of the ranch."

"Excuse me?" Joe didn't want to admit that he hadn't been paying attention, but it was the truth. "I missed the last part."

"I said, if the will you told Chloe about holds up, she'll inherit the ranch. It's in debt, but it has a lot of potential, and I know that the Cummings family would have wanted Dave's legacy to continue on. So you might want to consider using a portion of the life insurance benefits you're going to receive and offer her a loan so she can make a go of it."

"I'm sorry. Did you say benefits *I* would receive?"

"Yes, Mr. Wilcox. You're the sole beneficiary of Dave Cummings's five-hundred-thousand-dollar life insurance policy."

Joe almost collapsed on top of the stuff littering the bed. "But his death was... I mean, won't you need a death certificate?"

"I've already checked into that. The coroner ruled it an accidental overdose, which is a real shame." McDougall went on to explain that it would take some time to file everything properly and again suggested Joe work with Chloe to get the ranch back up and running.

"But does she even want the ranch?" Joe asked.

"Who's to say? I don't know many people who would take on that kind of responsibility even if it was forced on them. But Chloe Dawson is a sweet girl, and Teresa thought the world of her. It'll be hard for her to keep it, though. You definitely got the better end of the deal."

After the call ended, Joe's mind reeled with everything the attorney had disclosed. He reached for the picture of him and Dave, a somewhat goofy-looking guy who'd never stood a chance with Chloe.

Yet just hours ago, Joe had stood a damn good chance with the most kindhearted and beautiful woman in the world, and he'd thrown it away.

But he wasn't about to let her go without a fight. And he wasn't going to waste another minute in preparing for battle.

After checking on Ethel at the Brighton Valley Medical Center and having a chat with Dr. Nielson, Chloe had pulled into the parking lot of the Sheltering Arms and braced herself for a confrontation with the administrator. She was done hiding from arguments and was going to give him a piece of her mind.

So she marched right into Anthony J. Peabody's office and demanded to speak to him.

The slightly balding man looked up from his desk, rolled back his chair and crossed his arms. "Is this about losing your job?"

"No, it's about yours, Mr. Peabody—and Sarah Poston's. I warned you about her unprofessional behavior and her disregard for most of the patients, but you wouldn't listen to me. Instead, you got rid of me for being a squeaky wheel. But you won't get rid of me so easily this time."

"Is that a threat?"

"No, it's a promise. Ethel Furman is in the ICU right now, and it's all Sarah's fault."

"That's a pretty strong accusation. Ethel has pneumonia."

"Yes, and she also had a severe allergic reaction to the penicillin they gave her in the E.R. I warned Sarah about Ethel's allergy on several occasions and insisted that she order a new medical alert bracelet and that she note it in the chart."

"What did she say?" Mr. Peabody asked.

"That the bracelet was on order. And that her allergy was already noted in her chart. But rather than double-check to make sure, she refused to do so."

"Maybe someone in the E.R. didn't look at the chart that accompanied her in the ambulance."

Chloe crossed her arms. "I'm not sure what relationship you have with Sarah—familial or romantic—but you'd better stop trying to defend her without checking the facts. I spoke to Dr. Betsy Nielson just a few minutes ago, and she told me her allergy to penicillin definitely *wasn't* noted in the chart. Then she showed me herself. Sarah is guilty of lying or negligence. I suggest you figure out which one it is and deal with it—before Ethel's attorney contacts you about a lawsuit."

Mr. Peabody blanched, then swallowed—hard. "Ms. Poston and I aren't related in any way, shape or form. And I assure you that I'll check into your allegation."

"See that you do." Then Chloe turned on her heel and strode out of the admin office. Her steps didn't slow until she reached the lobby and spotted Joe chatting with several of the elderly patients who'd gathered near the Christmas tree in their wheelchairs or seated with their canes and walkers nearby.

She had no idea what Joe was doing here, but he'd better duck for cover because she was feeling pretty cocky after her last confrontation. And she wasn't the least bit concerned about having another blowup—even here in the lobby.

As she neared the older men, all of whom were military vets, she realized Joe was holding court and sharing war stories. Or so it seemed.

Sam Darnell was one of them, and while he looked especially lively seated with the other vets, she couldn't help her snippy tone when she addressed Joe. "What are you doing here?"

He got to his feet, but not with any of the bluster he'd had earlier. "I came to find you and apologize."

The wind should have died in her sails, but she was too angry and primed for battle to back down now. No simple apology would be enough to assuage the hurt she'd felt at being called a gold digger and being blamed for Dave's suicide.

"You're going to need to do a lot more than hang out with some of my friends, trading battlefield gossip to make up for the things you said."

"Battlefield gossip?" Sam swore under his breath. "I'll have you know that a war zone is no beauty parlor, missy."

She turned to the old cowboy, arms crossed. "I realize that. But Sergeant Wilcox shot a bazooka through my heart. Did he tell you about that?"

Sam aimed a furrowed gaze at Joe. "That true, son?"

Oh, how the tide was shifting. While these silver-haired vets might want to support a fellow marine, Chloe was the one who brought them their magazines and their favorite bakery treats.

Semper fi or not, if Joe didn't watch his step, he'd be facing a possible mutiny from his new cohorts.

"Yes," he admitted. "It's true. I said things out of misplaced anger and an emotion I'd never had to deal with before."

Ralph Mason, who refused to wash his WWII hat or replace it with a new one, leaned toward Joe. "You know, son, they have those PTSD programs over at the VA clinic. My nephew runs one of the support groups. You'd probably get a lot out of it."

"Thanks," Joe told him. "But I'm not talking about PTSD emotions, Ralph. I'm talking about love."

Chloe sucked in her breath. Did he just say what she thought he did?

Cliff Hawkins, a Korean War vet, chimed in. "My daughter joined one of those dating websites when her cheating ex-husband left her for that waitress over at that new cafeteria in Wexler. I'll bet they could help you find the right match."

Joe patted the wheelchair-bound vet on the knee. "That won't be necessary, Cliff. I already found the woman I love, although I have a whole lot of apologizing to do."

As he made his way toward Chloe, those amazing blue eyes zeroing in on her, turning her spine to mush and setting her heart on end, her anger dissolved. Only her wobbly knees supported her now.

Joe was within arm's reach when he said, "I just have

to convince her that she needs me just as much as I need her. And if she'll just give me a chance, I'll prove it."

"Ah hell," Ralph said. "Women don't need a man these days, son. What you gotta do is convince her that you'll love her no matter what and always buy her new dresses and promise to let her mother live with you, even when you hate the old biddy."

As much as Chloe wanted to scowl, she couldn't help smiling at the advice Joe's new cronies were giving him.

Nor could she tear her eyes away from the intensity and sincerity in his gaze.

He took her by the hand, and while her damaged ego and frail heart urged her to pull away, she didn't move a muscle.

"I love you," he said. "And I was a fool to think those awful things about you. And I was a real ass for saying them out loud. My amnesia was no excuse, but when all those memories came rushing back to me, I was overcome with all those old emotions I'd kept locked away. I didn't know who I was, but I do now. And I want to share that man with you—and let you know that he'll always stand beside you and always have your back."

Emotion clogged Chloe's throat, and she wasn't sure she could get the words out, even if she tried.

But the truth was, she'd seen the man Joe was talking about. She'd known he was there all along. And she wanted to trust him, to believe him.

But could she?

"Okay," Sam said, "Don't make the devil dog grovel, missy. Can't you just give him a second chance? If he lets you down again, he'll have to answer to me."

"He'll have to answer to all of us," Ralph said.

She almost choked on a laugh before George Eggleston added, "If Joe says he's sorry, you can believe it. Now go on and prove it to her, boy."

Before Chloe could respond, Joe followed the old man's advice and did just that, lifting her in his arms and kissing her with all the love he'd said he felt.

When they came up for air, she asked, "What about the ranch?"

"What about it? You can sell it or keep it—whatever you want. I now realize that you never really wanted it. Just know that I'll stand by whatever you decide to do. If you want to go back to nursing school, I'll even volunteer to let you practice poking me with hypodermic needles. I just want to be with you. I love you, Chloe Dawson."

Then he kissed her a second time while the men behind him erupted in cheers as if it was V-day all over again.

And that gave her pause—and the courage to broach the dream she'd kept hidden from him before.

"What about these guys?" she asked. "What if I wanted them to all come home and live on the ranch with us?"

Joe merely smiled, his eyes bright. "I've got the money to make that dream happen for you. Come to find out, I got an inheritance, too. So all you have to do is say the word."

"The word is I love you, too, Joe Martinez Wilcox." Then she kissed him again with all the love in her heart.

Epilogue

When Joe and Chloe arrived at Rick and Mallory's house for Christmas, their hosts opened the front door before they could even get out of the new truck Joe purchased to replace Ol' Greenie.

Just two weeks ago, he didn't even know he had a family. And now he was spending the holidays with his brother and sister-in-law, his nephew, and his soon-to-be fiancée—assuming Chloe said yes when she opened her Christmas gift.

As Joe reached into the back of the truck for their presents, Chloe carried a foil-covered pan up the sidewalk.

"What do you have there?" Mallory asked. "You didn't need to bring anything."

"Rick will want these," Joe said. "I used Tía Rosa's recipe. It won't be Christmas without them."

"You brought tamales?" Rick asked as he ushered them inside. His eyes lit up as he breathed in the spicy scent from the still-warm pan.

"I sure did."

Neither man mentioned the fact that most Christmases after their parents died hadn't been merry or bright. They'd often been ruined by their uncle's drunken escapades or alcoholic rants. But one thing they could always count on having were *Tía*'s tamales.

From what Joe had heard, their aunt and uncle's home was a happy one these days. So he planned to visit them sometime next week.

"I'd planned to bring some of my cranberry orange scones," Chloe told Mallory, "But Joe ate them all."

"Don't worry. Megan, Clay's wife, has been baking up a storm and brought a ton of desserts. Come on, I'll show you. She's in the kitchen, setting them out."

Joe had been looking forward to seeing Clay, his old high school buddy. He was also eager to meet Megan. He'd heard she was not only a fabulous cook, but had just launched her own line of homemade jams and preserves. There was talk of her opening a bakery, too.

"Did you hear what happened to drunk Larry?" Rick asked.

That was the driver of the Silverado that had hit Joe outside the Stagecoach Inn. "I knew his wife talked him into turning himself in right before Sheriff Hollister was going to make an arrest. And that he's out on bail."

"Apparently he decided to celebrate his freedom at a bar in Wexler two nights ago and was involved in another accident."

"No kidding? You'd think he would have learned his lesson."

"This time he hit a squad car driven by one of Wexler's finest," Rick said. "So it looks like he won't be driving or drinking for a while."

Joe was glad to hear that.

"Come on." Rick placed a hand on Joe's back. "Let's go find Clay."

"Good idea."

The reunion between the men—once three of Brighton Valley's most notorious outcasts—was soon filled with good-natured teasing and laughter. They didn't do much reminiscing, since none of them had the kind of past that had made Christmas special. But in true holiday spirit, they focused on the new blessings life had brought their way.

As Joe glanced around the crowded house, he saw that the kids were having a good time, too. His nephew Lucas, who actually did look a whole lot like him, had hit it off with Tyler, Clay and Megan's son. The boys sat near the tree, checking out their new video games and trying to decide which one to play first. And Lisa, Tyler's sister, was begging to go outside and try out her new soccer ball.

As Mallory passed out the eggnog, Rick stopped her long enough to pat her baby bump. A warm and tender moment passed between the obviously happy couple, which was enough to make Joe both grateful and envious at the same time. Maybe, if things went the way he hoped they would, he and Chloe would be adding to the Martinez clan one of these days.

"With the way the family is growing," Rick said, "we may have to move this party to the ranch next Christmas."

"I'd love that," Chloe said as she joined Rick near the hearth.

"Speaking of the ranch," Mallory said, "is the probate going okay?"

"Mr. McDougall seems to think it should move along without any snags. And once that's done, we should be able to start making changes to the ranch house and open the Brighton Valley Retired Cowboys' Home. We hope to welcome our first residents by spring."

"Actually," Joe said, "Sam Darnell, our first cowboy, will be moving in next week. He's a great guy. You'll have to come meet him. He'll be helping me learn the ins and outs of ranching."

"I never expected you to grow up to be a cowboy, Joey." Rick chuckled and gave him a brotherly nudge. "Of course, I never expected you to be a soldier, either."

"Why's that?" Joe asked.

"Because I wouldn't have thought you'd make it through boot camp."

"Well, I did. And if you think that was unbelievable, you're about to see a real miracle." He grabbed the wrapped box from beneath the tree and headed toward Chloe, who was seated on the sofa, talking to both Megan and Mallory.

Joe handed her the large gift with a bright red bow. "Merry Christmas, Chloe."

She looked at it in confusion, probably wondering when he'd had a chance to buy her anything. Then her gaze lifted to his. "But, Joe, I thought we weren't exchanging gifts until tomorrow morning."

Well, some of the things he'd bought her, like the black lace nightie he'd picked up at The Cowboy Connection in Houston, would have to wait until they were alone. But this was one he wanted to give her in front of his family and friends.

"I know," he said, "but indulge me and open this tonight." He stood before her and waited as she slowly removed the ribbon and unwrapped the box.

When she lifted the lid and spotted the red cowboy

boots she'd admired, her breath caught and a smile burst across her pretty face. "Joe, you remembered!"

He grinned, his heart swelling until he felt like the hero the military claimed he was.

"Try them on," he said.

"I'm sure they'll fit. Besides, I'd rather try them on at home."

"Please. Do it for me. I'd like to see how they look on you."

She balked one more time, but at his gentle urging, she removed her shoes. Then she slipped her foot partway into the right boot and frowned. "There must be cardboard or something shoved in there to keep the shape."

After removing her foot, she reached into the boot to retrieve whatever was stuffed inside, only to find a small, black velvet box. She gasped, then studied it in awe before realizing Joe had placed it there and had intended for her to find it.

By the time she flipped open the lid and spotted the sparkling diamond ring, Joe was down on one knee. "I love you, Chloe Dawson. Will you marry me?"

Her eyes sparkled, and she broke into a happy smile. "Yes!"

Then she wrapped her arms around his neck and kissed him, making a Christmas memory neither of them would ever forget.

* * * * *